NIGHT TERRORS

For Harry Parker

OXFORD
UNIVERSITY PRESS

Great Clarendon Street, Oxford OX2 6DP

Oxford University Press is a department of the University of Oxford.
It furthers the University's objective of excellence in research, scholarship,
and education by publishing worldwide. Oxford is a registered trade mark of
Oxford University Press in the UK and in certain other countries

First published 2019

Database right Oxford University Press (maker)

British Library Cataloguing in Publication Data
Data available

ISBN: 978-0-19-274998-7

1 3 5 7 9 10 8 6 4 2

Printed in Great Britain

Paper used in the production of this book is a natural,
recyclable product made from wood grown in sustainable forests.
The manufacturing process conforms to the environmental
regulations of the country of origin.

ALI SPARKES

NIGHT TERRORS

OXFORD
UNIVERSITY PRESS

CHAPTER 1

The beast lay on its side. Its shaggy red hide was frosted with new snow and one of its proud horns was driven into the heather. It looked as if it had been gently goring the hillside in its sleep. Whatever had made a hole right through it must have been fast. And surgically precise.

Jamie had never seen anything like this. The hole was perfectly round and the diameter of a large dinner plate. It should have been a mess of blood, broken ribs, and spilled organs—frozen into a gory cascade across the rough ground. But it was not. This tunnel through flesh and bone could have been made by some special effects wizard on a computer; it was as tidy as an edited picture.

Hamish went to sniff at it, whined, and ran back to press his rump against Jamie's legs, glancing up at his young master for reassurance. Jamie patted the collie's head and made a throaty noise of comfort, even though his own insides now felt tunnelled through with shock. What had *done* this?

His boots stayed rooted to the frostbitten turf and he instinctively did up the top button on his thick winter coat, pulling the scarf tucked inside it higher around his neck. The wind, moaning along Brawder's Pass, carried a bird of prey overhead. The raptor glided low, scanning for voles beneath the thin white icing of the valley, and then veered suddenly up and away as it reached the air above the dead cow.

Jamie took a steadying breath and went closer. The cow was six times his size and ten times his body weight, and seeing it felled like this was unsettling. He'd seen a dead cow before of course. Plenty of animals died out here in the bleak, long winters. But it was usually pretty clear on their corpses that they'd been attacked or scavenged by something he could identify; a fox or a wildcat or even, in some rare cases, an eagle. He had learnt what shapes these predators made in a carcass with their teeth, claws, beaks, or talons. He knew the pattern of their tracks. Uncle Fraser had taught him well.

He scanned the ground around the body for clues but found none. Nothing at all. No tracks, no crushing of the heather, no feather or fur snagged in the vegetation or the little craggy outcrop just above the kill zone. Anyway, why was he even looking? You could tell at a glance that nothing natural had happened to the dead animal.

Someone must have come up here with some kind of *machine*. They must have somehow sedated or killed the cow where it stood and then mutilated it in this bizarre way.

Jamie got down onto his knees and peered through the round window in the animal's flank. The inside was densely purple with streaks of red, brown, and ivory. The tunnel was as smooth as the inner curve of a clay pipe. He sat back on his heels and let out an exhalation of utter bafflement. Hamish crouched low in the snowy heather a short walk away, his ears flattened back; his eyes swivelling. Hamish did not want to look.

Jamie sympathized with the collie. This wasn't a picture anyone would want to dwell on. It was just too bizarre. It put him in mind of the Escher prints on the walls of the art room at school; strange, mathematical drawings of people walking up stairs which led down and around corners that floated in conflicting dimensions; of black and white swans forming a peculiar puzzle as they flew in and out of each other. The drawings always made him feel faintly sick. So did the window in the cow. It defied logic and made him wonder whether the problem was in his own eyes or brain . . . like a visual disturbance.

To be sure, he picked up his stick from where it had fallen and poked it through the cow to the other side. The stick tapped the rocky outcrop beyond. He withdrew it with a shudder, careful to avoid touching the carcass.

Time to go. Time to find Uncle Fraser and see if he could explain it. Jamie didn't have the first idea how he'd describe it—he'd have to draw it. Then he'd have to bring his uncle out here to see it for himself. He gave a low whistle and Hamish gratefully ran ahead of him, instinctively trotting for home.

Turning his back on the carcass Jamie suddenly felt his skin prickle with fierce goosebumps. Ahead of him Hamish's ears pricked up and his fur stood on end across his neck—but the dog didn't look back. It gave another whimper and ran on, faster.

He must be imagining it. He *must*. This was a Scottish Munro, not an Italian peak or a Japanese mountain. Nothing could make the ground tremble *here*. Nothing.

He decided it was just his own legs shaking. He was creeped out. Seriously. And now the overwhelming sense that he was *being watched* began to swamp him in panic.

Jamie did not glance back. He followed the instinct of his dog and ran.

CHAPTER 2

'Oh my god! Keep still. Tima ... don't move. There's something on your shoulder.'

Tima froze. Nineteen heads swung around as her fellow performers were alerted by Rowena's shrill voice. Rowena was a total drama queen (well, to be fair, they *all* were) and her loud, high delivery rang out across the auditorium; compressed calm with an undercurrent of panic.

'It's ... some kind of beetle.' Rowena visibly shuddered. 'Oh, it's in your hair! Don't panic. Someone get a cup or a bit of paper or ... eugh ...'

Tima tried to work out the best thing to do. If she made a grab for the little devil, it would maybe flutter out of her hair and freak out the entire cast. It was a good thing that they were in a break and Jonathon, the show director, had wandered off for a coffee. She'd only met him five days ago but she was pretty sure he wasn't an insect lover. He was temperamental on a *good* day, and she suspected he'd throw a total hissy fit if she went anywhere near him with her six-legged passenger. The best way was to negotiate but she and the beetle had only just met and her new friend was a bit unpredictable.

Tima turned and walked to the edge of the stage, gently placing her palm up by her shoulder and suggesting that the insect walk onto it. The beetle—a devil's coach horse, she was pretty sure—did so, but it was aggravated; raising its tail and making a scorpion shape.

Now there's no need for that, she sent to it, and at once the tail lowered. *What are you even DOING up here on a stage?* she went on. *Basements and bathrooms—that's more your thing, isn't it? Or a nice damp wood pile?*

'Have you got it? Is it dead?' Rowena had followed her.

'It's fine. It's just a beetle,' said Tima, holding out her flattened palm. 'They're called devil's coach horses. They can raise their tails like little scorpions,' she added, noticing that Rowena wasn't screaming and running away—and respecting her for it. *Go on,* she sent to the beetle, *show her.* It obligingly lifted its tail again.

'Wow,' said Rowena. 'Does it sting?'

'No,' said Tima, as the tail settled down again. 'But it's got a killer fart.'

Rowena shrieked with laughter and put her hands over her mouth.

Tima laughed too and turned to show the beetle to several

other cast members who had gathered around. 'It only farts if it's scared,' she said. 'So don't spook it. It'll squirt stinky stuff all over my hand if you do.'

'OK everybody, break over. Scene three!' Jonathon was back. He strode across to Tima and her little group of beetle watchers. 'Come on, you lot. Tima—what have you got there?'

Everyone stepped away and Tima held up the devil's coach horse with a cheerful smile. 'Just an interesting beet—'

'GAAAAAH!' yelped the fully-grown man. 'NOOO!' He backed away, looking horror-struck.

'It's OK, Jonathon, it's just . . .' Her little friend was alarmed and its tail had shot up again. 'Don't worry,' she said. 'I'll put it outside.' But as she went to walk past Jonathon, cupping the tiny creature in her hands, it edged out through a gap in her fingers and tumbled towards the stage, its stiff little wings helping it to glide . . . directly *on* to the maroon sleeve of the director's jumper.

The screaming was worthy of a death scene at the opera. Tima bit her lip and tried not to laugh as she went to collect the beetle, but it was difficult to catch because Jonathon was whirling his arms around in a panic.

'Just—wait—hold still . . .' she cried. Then things got even worse. A pungent stink was wafting from Jonathon's arm now. The beetle was doggedly clinging on and even burrowing down through the loose knit of the woollen sleeve.

Then, to top it all off, Jonathon gave a screech of pain. 'It just STUNG ME!'

Rowena stared accusingly at Tima. 'You said it didn't sting!'

'I know!' said Tima. 'But I didn't say it didn't *bite* . . .'

Then Jonathon fell backwards off the stage. He hit the swirly red carpet by the front row with a whump and lay there, dazed. Everyone shouted with alarm and raced towards him. Tima got there first and carefully collected the little devil from a hole in the man's sleeve. She enclosed it safely in her fist and ran for the back of the auditorium. As she shoved open the door to the foyer she found an assortment of parents sitting around, drinking coffee, waiting to collect their kids for tea.

Mum was there. She got to her feet as Tima paused in the doorway, the tableau of panic by the stage revealed before the heavy door could swing shut behind her. 'What's happening?' Mum asked.

'Back in a mo!' squeaked Tima and ran out into the cold December afternoon to deposit the beetle in the soil of a potted bay tree by the theatre steps. She didn't rush back in again. She sat down on the step, arms folded against the cold, and watched the beetle turn several circles and then burrow into the soil. *Thanks a bunch*, she sent to it. *Just as I was fitting in nicely*. She thought Jonathon was probably fine; just making a big drama out of it. Well . . . making a big drama out of things *was* his profession.

It was only when the ambulance pulled up and the paramedics ran in that she began to feel *really* guilty. She stayed on the chilly step and dropped her face into her hands. This whole Christmas theatre course was meant to be fun; a total holiday. She'd been having a great time. She hadn't been hanging out with insects *or* arachnids. Apart from a quick chat to a Chilean rose tarantula at Edinburgh Zoo, she'd been really good and kept focused on the *human* world.

Someone sat down next to her. 'I think we may need to have another little chat, Tima,' said Mum.

Tima sighed. 'It just landed on me,' she said. 'And then it flew off and landed on Jonathon. And he freaked out and fell off the stage. Is he . . . OK?'

Mum snorted. 'He's *fine*, I'm sure. They're just checking him for concussion but anyone who can make that much fuss can't be seriously injured. Come inside. You'll freeze out here.'

Jonathon *was* fine. The paramedics checked him over and decided he didn't need a trip to hospital. The cast finished for the day and everyone headed off with their parents, talking animatedly about the beetle attack which had nearly killed the director.

'Don't worry,' said Rowena, giving Tima a theatrical hug. 'It's not your fault. Nobody blames you.'

'Thanks,' muttered Tima. Glancing up at Mum, though, she wasn't so sure.

In the car Mum didn't say anything for a while and then, as they were negotiating their way across the tram tracks, past crowds of Christmas shoppers, she suddenly spoke up. 'How can you even *find* an insect in the middle of winter?' she said.

'Well, a devil's coach horse doesn't necessarily hibernate,' said Tima. 'And I didn't find it . . . it found me.'

Mum glanced across at her as she changed gear. 'It seems to me, if there is a spider, a beetle, an ant, or . . . even a scorpion . . . anywhere within fifty metres, it will find *you*. Why *is* that, Tima?'

Tima shrugged. 'Just lucky, I guess,' she said. Mum narrowed her eyes, but seriously, what else could Tima say? Every day she considered telling Mum the truth and every day . . . or more likely every night . . . she abandoned the idea.

She *could* tell her. She could tell her right now. 'Mum,' she could say. 'The thing is . . . I can *talk* to insects and arachnids. To all animals, really, but especially to the creepy-crawlies. I can ask them to do things for me and they do. They tell me stuff I need to know. They even pass messages on for me to Elena and Matt, back home. We're all like this, you see. We're all Night Speakers.'

And Mum would say: 'Night Speakers? What's a Night Speaker?'

And she would say: 'Well, Elena looked up our special powers online and she found this old legend about kids who could speak to animals if their parents left them out in the wilderness for a few nights just after they were born. If the babies didn't get eaten by wolves they gained the power to communicate with the animal world.'

And Mum would say: 'But we never left you out in the dark!'

And she would say: 'No—it's just a legend . . . but it kind of fits because it all started in the night. It all started with the insomnia . . . the beam . . .'

And Mum would say: 'Tima . . . I'm taking you back to the doctor.'

CHAPTER 3

The buzz and whine of the power planer told Jamie where to find his uncle. He sent Hamish off to find Hetty, Granddad's border collie, and wandered across to the low building nestled into the hillside a short walk down from the main house.

Like the house, it was old and made of stone, with a thick roof of ancient thatch and moss. Inside would have been dark with its small, deep-silled windows, but Uncle Fraser had painted the uneven walls white and attached spotlights to the rafters, so he had a bright space to work in. The floor was wooden and well maintained, as was everything above it. At one end of the long room was the workshop with its plane and lathe and other wood turning machinery. Uncle's well-kept carpentry tools were hung up on a grid on the furthest wall. Closer to the entrance was the area Jamie liked best—filled with beautifully-crafted chairs, tables, cupboards, and chests, awaiting delivery to customers all over Scotland—and sometimes beyond.

Often he would sit in a newly-made chair, tracing its elegant carvings, inhaling the scent of sap, hot sawdust, and beeswax while he watched his uncle work. He hoped to be able to make beautiful things from wood himself one day, but it would take a long time. He didn't have the coordination. His limbs were twisty and rebellious and his hands did not always obey his brain.

'Cold enough for you, out there?' yelled Uncle Fraser, not looking up from the smooth golden slab of oak he was working on at the plane. Jamie shrugged, perching on a wooden ottoman with brass hinges and a herd of leaping deer carved across its lid. Within its intricately worked oak frame on the wall, a mirror showed him a boy with a slouch to the left, mouth in a tight line; one cheek twitching. Uncle Fraser switched off the plane and blew the sawdust off his work. After a few moments he looked up at Jamie and furrowed his brow. 'What's up with you?' he asked.

'I found a cow with a massive hole in it,' said Jamie. At least that's what he wanted to say. What came out was far less clear.

'Wait . . . slow down,' said Uncle Fraser. 'You . . . you found something?'

Jamie nodded briskly and got up to mime a cow, using his forefingers to effect horns on either side of his forehead.

'You found a cow,' stated his uncle, raising a dark eyebrow. 'Well . . . there are roughly one point eight million cows in Scotland, so I guess it was always on the cards. Do you need a cup of tea for the shock?'

Jamie rolled his eyes and grunted with frustration. He held up both wonky hands and then pointed to his belly. Then he made a circular movement and stabbed both sets of fingers repeatedly at it.

'You're ... hungry ...' guessed Uncle Fraser. 'You want to eat a cow.'

Jamie stamped his feet and glowered and finally his uncle stopped messing around and paid attention to his *face*. Jamie opened his eyes wide and took a deep breath. If he really concentrated he could do this.

'H ... hole,' he said. The word exited his throat like a pitched lump of brick. 'In ... a ... cow.'

His uncle stepped over to him and rested two heavy hands on his shoulders. 'A hole ... in a cow? Is that what you mean?' His brow furrowed under his thick dark brown fringe. His eyes, the colour of the moss on the roof, narrowed. 'You found a cow ... with a *hole* in it?'

Jamie nodded again, frenziedly. In the mirror behind his uncle's shoulder his eyes were the same mossy green. If it weren't for a car accident when he was three he might have grown up to be as handsome as Fraser McCleod. But the accident had robbed him of his parents, most of his speech and any grace or speed he might have otherwise grown up to possess.

'Has a fox been at it? Or buzzards?' asked Uncle Fraser, tilting his head to one side and doing his best to intuit what his nephew was communicating. Jamie shook his head. He crouched down amid the fine sawdust on the floor. In it he drew a rudimentary cow shape, adding a circular hole in its belly.

'Really? A proper hole in it?' Both Uncle's eyebrows shot up this time. 'Well, this I have to see!'

The day was fading to dusk as they set out along the ridgeway towards Brawder's Pass. The knot in Jamie's stomach only got tighter as they got closer. *It's OK. You're with Uncle,* he told himself, but he couldn't shake the tense, pinched feeling.

It was about half an hour's walk, with a few climbs and scrambles along the way, and one road crossing. The main B road crested the ridge about halfway along their route and then zigzagged on down the glen towards a small hamlet called Ardlinney, which clung to the slopes just above the shores of Loch Braw. Not many people came out this way; it was mostly crofters at this time of year. Even so, he and his uncle were forced to wait on the thick heather verge beside the road while a shiny red Toyota 4x4 approached, its yellow beams picking out sparkling sleet as it swept past.

Uncle Fraser shook his head. 'Holidaymakers . . . in December! They're mad. One dump of snow and they'll be stuck here until spring!'

They moved on and eventually reached the rocky slope Jamie had wandered down with Hamish just an hour ago. Jamie felt the knot tighten further and he gripped his uncle's arm, pretending he needed to for balance on the slope. Beneath the small outcrop where he'd found the bizarrely mutilated carcass, Jamie saw . . . nothing. His mouth fell open.

He spun around, confused . . . angry.

'Are you sure it was here?' asked Uncle Fraser. 'It was

probably a bit further along.'

Jamie made a noise of frustration and shook his head vehemently. He stooped down and saw a pink stain across the thin snow. Some of the creature's blood must have seeped out of that neat, tidy wound after all. But where was the cow? Where?

Uncle Fraser crouched next to him. 'Aye, something was here. I can see how flattened the grass and the heather is . . . and that is blood. But whatever you saw here, something's come along and got it.'

Jamie screwed up his face. *What?* What could *possibly* have dragged away a massive lump of dead Highland cow? It would have weighed at least 500 kilos! Maybe if foxes worked in packs . . . or buddied up with some otters, some wildcats and a bunch of pine martens . . . like a scene from a very twisted Disney movie . . . maybe *then* they could move it. But he doubted it.

'I expect Peter Walker came by and collected it,' said Uncle Fraser. 'Got it up on the tractor trailer, with his two boys. Took it back to the fold so the vet could give it a post mortem. They do that, you know, sometimes . . . when the cause of death isn't obvious.'

The whacking great tunnel through its chest had looked pretty conclusive to Jamie . . . but there was nothing to show his uncle and in any case, it was getting too dark to look any further. Feeling inexplicably furious, Jamie turned and trudged back up the hillside, shoving his gloved hands deep into his coat pockets. He might have told his uncle about the shaking ground too . . . *if* they had found the holey cow . . . but now it would just make him look even stupider than he already was. And that was a lot.

CHAPTER 4

A light snow was falling as Tima stepped outside in her swimsuit. With a squeak she ran across the deck and threw herself, shivering, into the water.

'Oooooooh yeah,' she sighed as she drifted down into the bubbles. 'This . . . is . . . officially . . . heaven.' She lay back in the hot tub and let the churning whirlpool push her legs up to the surface, delighting in the sensation of pummelling heat up to her neck and icy kisses across her face as the snowflakes landed and melted. Close to the deck a small Norwegian spruce gave off a gorgeous scent that was pure Christmas. The owners of Loch View Luxury Lodges had decorated it with strings of coloured lights.

Mum and Dad were not religious. They'd moved to the UK from Yemen, many years ago, leaving much of their Arab culture behind. They didn't intend to adopt any Christianity either, but they did enjoy the Christmas festival and, as Mum pointed out, much of it was based on ancient pagan celebrations anyway. So they happily got a tree in each year and bought presents for their daughter and each other. This year they would celebrate their borrowed festival in the Scottish Highlands.

The musical theatre course ran from the first week in December right to the end of the year and into the first week of January. It stopped, of course, for Christmas Eve, Christmas Day, and Boxing Day . . . and then the show began on December 28 and ran, pausing for New Year's Eve, through to January 3. Six nights of performance across the holidays—to a packed theatre filled with families and friends. Or so she'd been told.

'I was on it last year,' Rowena had informed her, the first day they'd all met at the theatre. 'It was a sell out! It always is. Jonathon, the director, normally works on shows in the West End—all his famous theatrical friends come up to see it!'

It *was* an internationally renowned course; a spur of the National Youth Music Theatre in London. The auditions were tough . . . and then there was the cost. Mum and Dad hadn't said how much it was, but Tima knew it was a pretty eye-watering sum. The costumes for *Winter Storm*—a Medieval Christmas musical—were being borrowed from the Royal Shakespeare Company. The scenery was a work of art. A man had come to the theatre to build the sets out of wood and paper. He hadn't just knocked it all up, though—he was actually *carving* stuff in the wings as they all rehearsed; chiselling out leaves on trees and blades of grass along the bottom of the flats.

Tima rested her head on the smooth edge of the tub and gazed up into the wooden eaves that hung over the deck to shield hot tub funsters from the worst of the weather. A small orbweb spider was huddled up there next to one of the golden outdoor lamps. *How do you manage out here . . . in all this . . . weather?* she asked it, idly.

What is weather? it seemed to answer. Of course, to a Scottish spider, this cold was just . . . normal.

Can't be much to eat out here, she observed. The spider wasn't chatty but it was curious about her. It abseiled down and would have landed in her hair except the patio door suddenly slid open and Mum came out, wrapped up in a fluffy towelling dressing gown, and ran for the tub.

No—don't! Quick—go back up! Tima sent. Her new friend stopped, swung for a second in the breeze, and then zoomed back up its throwline before scuttling away behind the light fitting. Tima vowed to herself to *stop* befriending arachnids and insects, at least for the length of her holiday. She missed Spencer, the friendly house spider who lived in her bedroom, but there really was no reason to invite more awkward chats with Mum.

'Oh yes . . . this is the life!' said Mum as she sank into the hot tub. 'Glad we got this place, now?'

'Oh yes,' said Tima. 'Better than a boring hotel.' Both she and Dad had queried the wisdom of booking a luxury lodge more than an hour's drive from Edinburgh but Mum had insisted she wanted to experience the *real* Scotland, up in the mountains.

'But we might end up experiencing a *real* Scottish *blizzard,*'

Dad had pointed out.

'So . . . we'll keep an eye on the forecast and book into a hotel in Edinburgh if it looks like a blizzard is on the way,' Mum had argued. And when she'd shown them their Loch View lodge they hadn't argued any further. It was gorgeous; a converted old crofter's hut, with skylights and stripped wooden floors, deerskin rugs and a cast iron wood burner. The kitchen had every mod con you could want and there was a *cinema room* with all the top broadband channels and a massive screen that would roll down the wall at the touch of a button. The only thing missing from this perfect place, Tima realized, were her two best friends.

Elena and Matt were back in Thornleigh, having a more ordinary December; in school until halfway through the third week and then doing the usual Christmas stuff at home. Nothing much else was going on. She wondered if they would still meet up in the tree house in the woods each night without her; it was getting very wintry and even the paraffin heater was struggling to keep the cold at bay. But they would still be awake, even if they didn't go out, for four or five hours across the night. Insomnia was what connected them all. Up here, far from Thornleigh, far from the beam which sang through her bedroom every night on the dot of 12.34 a.m. (or 1.34 a.m. in British Summer Time), Tima had been sleeping better. Up here, though, she instinctively opened her eyes at precisely the same time, wondering why there *wasn't* a beam rushing through her world. It felt odd to her; as if she might be missing out on something important . . . but she could usually get back to sleep in an hour. And with all the acting and singing and dancing she was doing in the daytime, it was just as well. She needed her sleep.

'Dad's cooking,' Mum sighed, looking the picture of bliss on the other side of the hot tub, her dark hair floating across the water and her eyes closed. 'We're having lamb saltah . . .'

Tima could already smell the spices and the frying meat. 'Not too much garlic,' she said. 'I'll be breathing it all over the cast tomorrow.'

'Ha!' said Mum. 'It'll do them good. Oooh—look. The stars are out!'

The light dusting of snow had stopped, Tima realized, and the sky had cleared. Pinpricks of starlight shone out and a half moon was mirrored in the dark, still loch. The diamond-shaped body of water lay a ten or fifteen minute downhill walk from their lodge. 'This is such a great spot,' Tima said. 'We've got the best lodge!'

There were another five lodges dotted around the site, two converted from old stone cottages, like theirs and three built of wood. Each dwelling had its own twinkling Christmas tree growing outside. Fairy lights were also wound along the fencing beside the drive down from the car park. It was very pretty in the light snow. The website said a tractor was on hand to tow cars up to the main road in the event of heavy snow but the forecast hadn't warned of any.

The patio door slid open again and Dad peered out, wearing a striped apron. 'Food will be on the plate in ten minutes,' he said.

'Shall I come in and help?' asked Mum.

'That would be good,' said Dad. 'Although I see you're nearly simmered to perfection yourself!'

Mum laughed and clambered out of the tub, squeaking as the cold hit her. She grabbed her robe and threw it on. 'Five more minutes, Tima!' she said. 'Then come in and get dry and lay the table, OK?'

'OK,' said Tima, floating dreamily.

The patio door slid shut again and she flipped onto her front, kicking across the pool to rest her arms and chin on the wooden outer ledge and gaze down into the valley. She let out a long, contented sigh.

What she saw next made her suck it back in again in shock.

One moment the surface of the loch lay still, like solid pewter. The next moment a well appeared, right in the centre, as if someone had suddenly pulled out a plug beneath, the water plunging smoothly downward. Then, as Tima stared, open mouthed, the whole thing inverted—a perfectly round funnel shot high into the air and then splashed down with enough impact that she felt the shockwave of displaced air blow into her face three seconds later.

'Wha . . . ?' she gasped out, eyes wide as a small tsunami sped in concentric circles across the water. How high it was she could not tell from this distance, but she could make out white froth as the waves hit the shore—and hear the water crash against pebbles and rocks, rebounding back across the loch in ragged waves.

She flung herself out of the hot tub and ran inside to tell her parents, throwing the towel around her.

But by the time they'd come out there was nothing to see

except ripples fanning out across the loch.

'It was probably just a big fish,' said Dad.

'Or maybe an otter,' said Mum.

'Or maybe the Loch Ness Monster . . . here on its holidays!' teased Dad.

Tima shoved his shoulder. 'Don't laugh at me! It was big. Really *big!*'

'Come on—get in and get yourself dry and dressed before you get a chill,' said Mum.

Tima went back in to do just that. She took a deep breath and told herself to relax. *She was on holiday.* She was far, far away from all the dramas of Thornleigh. Nothing weird or life-threatening was going on this time.

It was all fine.

Just fine.

CHAPTER 5

'Can you pass me the chisel?' Uncle Fraser grunted, crouched down on the matte black surface of the stage. Jamie did so, quickly. He knew his uncle's bag of tools inside out; he'd been helping him with carpentry work for as long as he could remember. Sometimes Jamie did bits of work himself, but there had been quite a lot of accidents over the years; quite a lot of bleeding on some nice wooden shelves or a beautifully turned newel post.

Uncle Fraser never told him off; he always congratulated him for trying, in fact, but Jamie's brain and limbs would never co-operate for long no matter how hard he focused. There would always be a sudden jerk . . . or a spasm . . . or a lurch to the left. In fact *Lurch* was his nickname at school. Among other things. He'd never been able to come back with a quick counter-insult when the usual lads decided to pick on him, but he had learned, over many years, a great repertoire of rude gestures. You had to defend yourself any way you could at school, especially now he was in S2 and surrounded by increasingly moody teenagers.

Back in primary, things had been OK. He couldn't talk well enough for most people to understand and he walked, according to his uncle, 'like a cheerful zombie', so he didn't have many friends. His work wasn't bad. His handwriting was appalling but once the teacher had learned to read it, it turned out he was quite bright.

Ullochry High, though, had been a whole new experience. More than 800 kids were bussed in every weekday, from miles around. It wasn't the gentle environment of the primary school, though, and even before the end of his first day he'd been nicknamed Lurch . . . and not in an affectionate way.

Sometimes he played up to it. He had been known to lurch 'accidentally' right into the faces of kids who called him names. He'd never tried to punch one of them; he could never be sure his fist wouldn't just travel up and hit his *own* face. But he was very good at falling on people and seemed to have an uncanny knack for landing an elbow where it hurt. And then burbling out: 'Sooorrrrry,' in his most cheerful zombie voice. He refused to be a victim.

'That's a really lovely bit of scenery.' Both Jamie and his uncle twisted around and looked up at a girl of about ten or eleven who was standing a few steps away, pulling her long dark hair up into a scrunchie.

'Thank you,' said Uncle Fraser, smiling. Jamie just smiled. It was nice to give the illusion of normality for as long as he could.

'Did *you* do all the carving?' asked the girl, coming closer and running her fingers along the leaves and acorns that had been worked into the wooden trees at this side of the stage.

'Aye,' said Uncle Fraser. 'Although *carving* is probably overstating it. They're pretty rough work, really. I've not got time to finish them to a very high standard.'

'They're beautiful,' said the girl. 'And they look fantastic from the auditorium—almost like real trees! Do you both work on them?'

Jamie laughed and answered before he thought better of it. 'I just hand the genius his tools,' he said. *Why* was he speaking? He sounded like a total bampot. At any moment she was going to start backing away with a tight smile; *retreat, retreat from the weirdo!*

But to his immense surprise, she looked right at him and said, with mock gravity: 'Well, somebody's got to pass the chisel. I bet you do it better than anyone else.'

'He's learning the trade too,' said Uncle Fraser, getting up and dusting down his overalls, smiling even more deeply at the girl, because she was making an effort for his nephew, Jamie guessed. The girl was pretty and graceful—a dancer, going by her soft leather shoes and leggings. She was posh too; beautifully spoken; the kind who'd normally steer well clear of someone like him.

'Learning the trade?' echoed Jamie, laughing. 'The only thing I'm safe with is sandpaper . . . and I could probably still wreck a bookcase with it . . . given enough time.' And he let his wonky arms spasm for comedic effect.

The girl hooted with laughter. He blinked. She had totally *got the joke*. She had *understood* him! How? Even Uncle Fraser would have struggled to work out everything he'd just said; it had come out of his awkward mouth at such speed. Ah, but more likely she was just laughing politely. She'd back away now.

'I've seen you both before, haven't I?' she said, suddenly stretching a leg up to one side, without any self-consciousness, and pointing her toes towards the lighting rigs above.

They glanced at each other, surprised. 'Have you?' said Uncle Fraser.

'Yes . . . you were up at Loch View, where we're staying, mending the decking last week. You had a black-and-white dog with you.'

'Yeah . . . Hamish,' said Jamie. 'He's my border collie.'

'Hamish! Great name for a dog!' she said, stretching up the other leg.

Uncle Fraser was glancing at him now, a warm and slightly baffled look on his face. He was clearly delighted that his nephew was having a conversation; he was also pretty amazed that the girl could understand it.

'TIMA! Come ON!' yelled the director and the girl shrugged, gave them both a little wave, and skipped back to the rehearsal.

'Take care, Sandpaper Boy!' she called back, over her shoulder.

'Well, that was . . . unusual,' said his uncle.

Jamie listened to his own words as they rolled out as thick

and lumpy as ever: 'Shfee oonsoood ma.'

'She *did* understand,' marvelled his uncle. 'Fancy that . . .'

They got on with checking the scenery Uncle Fraser had built; fine-tuning some of the rougher carvings and working the hinges and the castors; crucial for folding and rolling the flats away smoothly and silently during scene changes. Some flats were simple frames stretched with canvas and painted; others were the more intricate work his uncle was renowned for.

An hour later the rehearsal was winding up for the end of the day with one final song. Jamie listened to the girl singing a solo. It was quite the most beautiful thing he'd ever heard. Jamie had always longed to sing—but his attempts sounded like Granddad's bull getting an injection from the vet.

When she finished he had to put down the tool bag and clap. His ragged, slappy applause rang across the stage above the polite ripple from the rest of the cast. She glanced across and he felt himself go crimson with embarrassment. Everyone looked at him and then several of them were pulling faces at each other as they gathered up their bags and changed into outdoor shoes.

'Come on, Jamie,' said his uncle, putting a hand on his shoulder. 'We've got to go too.'

They packed the tools away and shrugged their winter coats on as the stage rapidly emptied; kids running up through the auditorium to meet parents who were waiting in the foyer. Uncle Fraser went to tell the stage manager they were done for the day and Jamie was just wondering whether to ask if they could come back and see the show when someone tapped him on the shoulder.

'Hey, Sandpaper Boy!' She was back, her coat on and her bag slung over her shoulder. 'Do you live near Loch View?'

He nodded. 'Half an hour away on foot.'

She nodded as if she understood every clunky syllable.

'So . . . did you see that thing in the lake? I mean . . . the loch . . . last night?'

He frowned, thinking. 'What thing?'

She shrugged, laughing. 'It's probably nothing. I mean . . . maybe it happens all the time. It just looked so weird . . .'

'What?'

'Well . . . it looked like someone had pulled the plug out in the middle of it. All of a sudden there was this perfectly round hole in the water . . . and then it all shot up like a fountain. And then . . . well . . . it just went back to normal, I suppose.'

Jamie hadn't seen anything like it – but even so, something made goosebumps wash all over his skin.

'Perfectly round . . .?' he said. 'It was . . . *perfectly round*?'

'Yup. Like a plug hole . . . have you seen that before?'

He shook his head.

'Ah well . . . never mind. See you.' And she ran back across the stage before he could say another word.

He shivered, thinking of the *perfectly round* hole in the cow. Could that be connected to a perfectly round hole in the loch? *Oh come on!* he told himself. *That's really not likely, is it?* But it seemed to be a day for unlikely things because he'd actually met someone, for the first time, who totally *understood* him.

That was even freakier than the holey cow.

CHAPTER 6

Are you awake?

Tima's eyes pinged open as her mobile phone buzzed on the bedside table. She hadn't really been asleep, just dozing. She'd woken up at 12.34 a.m. on the dot, realized the beam wasn't coming through because she was 400 miles away from Thornleigh, felt that odd combination of relief and disappointment, and then started to drift off again. Until now.

Getting up on her elbow, she fumbled for the phone and pressed it into life. It was just after two in the morning and the text was from Elena.

Yes! What's happening? she texted back, quickly. A hot surge of adrenalin reminded her that she was probably not really over the events of the past few months. And who would be? She and Matt and Elena had been through some stuff that nobody else on the planet could understand; they'd fought off an underworld god with massacre on its mind, battled against an alien with a plan to overtake the Earth using deadly oxygen-sucking plants—and even foiled an interplanetary kidnap plot.

Without their Night Speakers powers they most certainly couldn't have succeeded . . . they'd all be dead by now if the animal world hadn't come to their aid every time. But what now? Was something ELSE coming for Thornleigh? Was something new travelling through the beam and into their world from another dimension?

Bzzzz. **Nothing much. Just bored. It's too cold to hang out in the treehouse. Matt's round at mine.**

Matt was at Elena's—in the middle of the night? Tima remembered that Elena's mum slept very heavily thanks to the drugs she had to take for her bipolar condition. She could picture Matt and Elena now, sitting by Elena's bedroom window, drinking hot chocolate and watching the world go by.

Say hi 2 Matt for me. I miss u both! And Lucky . . . she texted back, sitting up in bed, fully awake now.

Bzzzz. **Ha! I bet you don't miss the insomnia. How many hours are you getting up there?**

Tima grinned and decided to risk a call. The walls of the old cottage were very thick; she could probably get away with it. Mum and Dad would be sound asleep. Elena picked up immediately. 'I'm sleeping like a baby!' Tima said, in a low voice. 'Well . . . except for at the moment, obviously.'

'Are you still waking up at the usual time?' Elena asked.

'Yeah—it's weird. There's no beam and nothing strange

going on . . .' she paused, thinking of the loch, and then dismissed it. It really *wasn't* strange. Not compared to what she and her friends had seen this year. 'I guess I'm just so used to waking up at the same time that my body clock is still ticking on in the same way. But I usually go to sleep again pretty soon. And it's just as well—the director of *Winter Storm* is making us work so hard.'

'How's the show going?' came Matt's voice, and Tima realized she was on speaker at the Thornleigh end.

'Brilliantly!' breathed Tima. 'I've got a solo to sing at the end. And the dance stuff is going really well—they let me choreograph some of it because I'm the best dancer! Anyway, how about you? How's life in Thornleigh? Have you finished school yet?'

Matt groaned. 'No. We've got another week. Only posh schools like yours close for Christmas for a whole *month*. It's not fair.'

Tima thought she heard a small echo of Matt's heartfelt *'It's not fair.'*

'Is Lucky with you?' she asked, suddenly missing Matt's friendly starling as much as her two human friends.

'Yeah,' said Matt. 'Although she should be asleep in a tree somewhere. I've got to stop keeping her up at nights.'

'So,' cut in Elena. 'Everything's OK with you? You're having fun?'

'Yes! You should see the lodge we're staying in. It's got a hot tub!'

Matt groaned again. 'Remind me to be born a rich kid next time around,' he muttered.

'Have you seen anything of Spin?' Tima asked.

'No,' said Elena. There was a pause, during which Tima pictured the pale, lean figure of Spin, their sometime friend and sometime enemy. He roamed the streets of their town by night, a self-styled vampire. He was seriously strange . . . the first time Tima had met him he'd chased her and terrified her. But he *had* helped them more than once in a crisis. Tima couldn't decide how she felt about him these days.

'Tima—' began Elena, but then Tima heard a thud beyond her bedroom door and realized either Mum or Dad had got up and gone into the kitchen. She heard the muffled gurgle of the tap being run.

'Sorry,' she hissed. 'Parent alert! Have to go. Will call again soon, OK?' She ended the call and put the phone back on her bedside table. Not a moment too soon, as Mum's dark silhouette appeared around the door. Tima pretended to be asleep and Mum tilted her head. Tima sensed, rather than saw, her smile. And then Mum was gone. Tima sneaked one more look at her phone and saw Elena's final text: **It's OK. Sleep well and have a great time. X**

'You should have told her!' Matt sprawled back on her bed, Lucky perched on his right knee. He looked worried.

'Look—I don't think we need to say anything,' said Elena. 'She's having such a great time. She's sleeping and singing and dancing . . . I don't want to worry her for no reason. I mean . . . we don't *know* that it's anything to worry about, do we?'

Matt got up and went to the window. Everything in the

lamplit street looked pretty normal. If you discounted the two massive golden eagles sitting on the roof of the house opposite, staring right at him.

'They've been there for ages now,' said Elena. 'When are they going to come and talk to you?'

Matt shrugged. 'I'm going to send Lucky out to them again.' He held the starling up on his fist as Elena opened the window wide. 'See if you can get some sense out of them this time,' he said and his feathered friend echoed: *'Sense!'* and flew out.

They watched as her small silhouette flitted above the dim street. Matt took a slow breath, telling himself not to worry. Yes . . . she could be easy prey to two such massive raptors, but he had never yet seen any predator strike when it was in company with a Night Speaker.

In the thin light thrown up by the street lamps the golden eagles looked like avenging angels; hunched shadows on the ridge of the roof. Matt saw their heads move sharply as Lucky fluttered close by; he could sense their tension. He knew they were here to warn him about something . . . maybe even to ask for help. But he couldn't work out why. The images and sensations they sent were vague and spinning . . . there was nothing he could recognize through the loose weave of telepathy he got from the bird world.

The eagles had arrived earlier that evening, circling Kowski Kar Klean while he worked on a Citroën before dinner. He'd heard their high, piercing cries high overhead and instantly knew they had come to see him. But he'd had to tell them to hold off—to wait until well after midnight when he would be free to speak to them. Dad was close by and he wasn't in a good mood. There was a bruise on Matt's left cheekbone, slowly swelling, which Dad would deny all knowledge of if anyone ever asked. Getting ten minutes off work to get into a nearby wood and communicate with a pair of golden eagles really wasn't an option.

All the way to Elena's house in the early hours he was aware of the pair flying low, occasionally landing on rooftops and telegraph poles, then flapping up and on, following his route. It was not easy for such huge birds to fly in the dark; they normally depended on the thermals rising from the land in the daylight hours to keep them aloft.

He'd felt bad about keeping them waiting until so late into the night but there was no way he could have talked to them while he was at home. A starling in his room was one thing—a couple of raptors with two metre wingspans was something else. Even on the journey to Elena's he'd held them off. He needed to be able to slip away into the dark shadows whenever late night motorists drove by . . . and again, with a golden eagle on each arm, that just wasn't possible.

Once at Elena's he'd gone into her room and they'd thrown open the window . . . but the eagles wouldn't fly in. He couldn't blame them—a bird used to hunting across mountains and plains would never fly into a small, dark space—not even with two Night Speakers waving them in like air traffic control.

Instead, they sat on the roof and sent their message of spinning fear.

Lucky flew back in. She landed back on Matt's fist and fed him the same intel. The eagles had seen something that was terrifying them . . . in endless circles.

'I need to get them to fly to me,' he said to Elena. 'Lucky—go and tell them to come into the back garden. We'll be waiting.'

They moved silently past Callie's room, aware of her even, deep breathing. Matt often wondered what Elena's mother would do if she ever came out and found her daughter with a teenage boy in her room. Although they were friends—very *good* friends—there was nothing else going on, but it would be difficult to explain.

Downstairs, they slipped silently out of the house into the shadow of the back garden and waited.

The eagles arrived with a substantial downdraft. Matt did not hold out a fist for them to land on. The female had to weigh as much as a small dog. The pair landed heavily on the curved wooden back of a garden bench. In the dim light that shone out from Elena's kitchen window, they were fiercely beautiful, with russet feathers across their heads and yellow-ringed dark eyes above viciously-curved beaks.

'You've come all the way from . . .' he paused and closed his eyes. '. . . Scotland. Why?'

They gazed at him fixedly and the male made a soft hissing noise. Matt smiled, suddenly realizing they had met before. 'You helped us back in the autumn, didn't you?' he murmured, a flash of memory in his mind. The male flashed it right back at him; both of them fighting a common foe on the roof of Thornleigh's highest tower block.

'I never did say thank you,' said Matt. 'So . . . thank you.'

'Why has he come back?' asked Elena, wiping a pale strand of hair off her face and gazing at the bird in awe. 'Maybe he can make the message clearer now we're so close. Should you . . . maybe . . . touch him?'

Matt glanced at her and then back at the pair of raptors, their killer talons clenched on the back of the bench. These were not the kind of birds you petted. But it might help to make physical contact. Tentatively he stretched out his hand, expecting the eagles to hiss and maybe even bite. But they didn't.

Is this OK? he sent out to them. And they sent back: *It is.*

His fingers rested lightly on the male's head and then his other hand found the feathered crown of the female. Both were thrumming with energy and as soon as he made contact he could sense how deeply troubled they were. Exhausted too, with their long journey down from the mountains and the enforced night flying.

But more than any of this, he suddenly knew something was shaking their world; spinning it apart. Something so frightening it had driven two of the avian world's biggest, most efficient predators to fly hundreds of miles to ask him, a teenage boy in the backwater town of Thornleigh, for help.

There was something else too. Some*one* else. Matt felt a chill run through him as he double-checked with the female. Maybe he had imagined it. *Did you . . . did you mean to show me Tima?* The female hissed her confirmation. Something huge and horrifying was happening . . . and Tima was in the middle of it.

Matt turned to Elena. 'We have to go to Scotland,' he said. 'Tonight.'

CHAPTER 7

A wild, high-pitched scream jolted Tima out of sleep. She was sitting up, heart racing, in an instant. Her bedside clock showed 4.23 a.m. What the *hell* was that noise?

She got up and padded to her window, pulling the thick tartan curtain aside to peer out. The lodge's Christmas lights twinkled and sent a glow across the darkness but she couldn't make out any shape or movement. *Seriously, girl—it was just a dream. Get a grip.* Or it could have been a fox ... maybe even a wildcat. They could be a bit screamy at times.

A spider was nestled up against the curtain pole. *Is there anything I should be worried about?* she asked it. The spider just turned a circle and settled back into its corner. It didn't seem relaxed ... but it didn't seem scared either. Spiders weren't really very communicative, to be honest. Spencer, back home, was a bit of an exception.

She was about to get back into bed when she noticed golden light shafting under the door. She put on her warm dressing gown and went out into the hallway. The light was coming from the kitchen and now she could hear low voices murmuring. She pushed open the door and found Mum and Dad sitting at the table with hot drinks.

'Oh, I'm sorry, lovely,' said Mum. 'Did I wake you?'

'Um . . . no . . . I don't think so,' said Tima. 'Just got up for a drink.' She was pretty sure her mother couldn't make a scream like she'd heard in her dream. 'What's up?'

'I had a weird dream,' said Mum. 'I dreamt the room was shaking. I woke up all panicky—convinced there was an earthquake.' She laughed and shook her head.

'Like being back in Yemen,' said Dad, cupping his mug. 'We got them all the time there,' he added, nodding at Tima. 'Once or twice a month.'

'They used to terrify me,' said Mum. 'All the animals would start running and if you knew what was good for you, you'd run along with them. They say animals always know which way to run,' she went on. 'Once, me and my two brothers had to sleep under a table, our mother was so scared. There had been a big quake the day before in a village only an hour's walk from us and we had felt it. She was convinced it would happen right under our house. These quakes . . . they travel, you know. Along fault lines.'

'Was that why you moved to England?' asked Tima.

'No—it was for your father's job,' said Mum. 'He was

headhunted—because he is a brilliant surgeon.' She smiled at her husband.

'And you're a brilliant vet, Mum,' added Tima.

'That's right,' said Dad. 'Your mother—' He broke off suddenly, put down his coffee, and stood up, narrowing his eyes as he gazed across the room. Tima and Mum followed the direction of his gaze to the wall and both gave a murmur of surprise.

'Was that there before?' asked Dad.

Mum went to the wall. It was solid stone but had been rendered with a rough plaster finish and painted a luminous white. There was a deep black crack running across it from ceiling to floor.

'No,' said Mum, looking mystified. 'I'm sure I would have noticed that.' She turned to stare, baffled, at Dad. 'You don't think I felt an *actual* earthquake, do you?'

'What—here—in the Scottish Highlands?' Dad laughed. 'No . . . more likely the steam from the hot tub has just got into the plaster. Or even more likely, it *was* there before and we've only just noticed it thanks to your earthquake nightmare!'

'You *can* get earthquakes here,' said Tima. 'We did it in geography. Britain has about 200 earthquakes a year. Most of them are too small to notice, but sometimes they're big enough to shake a picture off the wall.'

Mum looked shocked. 'Well . . . to think we came here for some relaxation!'

Dad shook his head. 'There is *no way* we had an earthquake. It was just a dream. Come on—we all need to get back to bed.

OK, Tima?'

Tima nodded, getting herself a glass of water. Back in her bed she lay staring at the ceiling for some time. She felt rattled. The scream in her dream . . . Mum talking about earthquakes . . . the crack in the wall. *Had* it been there before? She couldn't be sure.

She thought about texting Elena but then decided she didn't want to worry her friend. What if she'd just managed to get back to sleep? Elena and Matt really needed their sleep—they wouldn't thank her for waking them up for no good reason.

She closed her eyes and pictured her best friends snuggled up in their beds, slumbering peacefully. Just where they should be. Sleeping and safe.

CHAPTER 8

'The Mercedes E class would get us there quickly,' whispered
Matt. 'It's got a powerful engine and was built for speed . . . but
the Land Rover Discovery has nearly a full tank and it'll be
good for off-roading.'

Elena let her heavy backpack drop to her feet as Matt
weighed up which car to steal. She couldn't quite believe she was
agreeing to all of this. She was, though. She was agreeing. Those
two eagles just couldn't be argued with. As they watched them
flap away into the dark, she and Matt both knew it. She'd made
Matt wait for ten minutes while she threw some sandwiches
together and packed them in her bag with crisps and biscuits
and a flask of hot chocolate. Then she'd written a note to her
mum. Then they'd gone, jogging through the pre-dawn to Matt's
place.

'The Merc owner will probably call the police sooner,' Matt went on. 'The Disco owner's pretty laid-back—he might wait a while if Dad spins some story about a cracked windscreen or something. Sometimes the pressure jet kicks up a bit of gravel and a windscreen cracks—Dad gets a bloke he knows to fix it.'

'Won't your dad just report it as stolen?' Elena whispered back.

'Maybe not if he knows his son was the thief,' said Matt.

'You're going to *tell* him?' Elena gaped at her friend, her eyes resting on the swelling on his cheek. 'He did *this* just because you forgot to clean a cupholder. What is he going to do after you nick a client's car?!'

Matt shrugged. He led her into the small office area where all the car keys were kept on a row of hooks behind the desk and selected the Land Rover key. Then he grabbed a bit of paper and scribbled a note.

It read: Mum & Dad—had an emergency. Need to help a friend. Had to take the car. Please don't worry. I will see you soon. Matt x

'What will they do?' breathed Elena as they went back out to the Land Rover. She could see Matt was holding it all in but he must be terrified. The punishment he would get didn't bear thinking about . . . if Elena didn't know that Tima was in terrible danger she would never let him do this.

'I don't know,' said Matt, quietly opening the driver's door. 'I don't care whether my old man blows a gasket or sits on the floor and cries like a baby. I *do* care about Mum, though.' He gulped and then shook his head. 'Dad doesn't hit her,' he said, more to himself than Elena. 'She'll be OK.'

Lucky dropped onto his shoulder from her perch on his bedroom windowsill. She was intent on coming with them. 'She'll be OK,' she echoed.

Matt put the Land Rover into neutral and took off the handbrake, so it rolled quietly off the sloped forecourt and some way down the road. Then he turned the key and the engine started up. He was way too young to be driving, of course, but he'd needed to do it several times this year. Elena worried that he was breaking the law, but the good people of Thornleigh had a lot to thank him and his criminal behaviour for. Getting the Night Speakers where they needed to be fast had saved many lives over the past few months. Thousands, if not millions. It was a shame nobody aside from Elena, Tima, a pseudo vampire, and a couple of aliens would ever know.

'You're getting good at this,' observed Elena as they headed north-east on the dual carriageway.

'Well at least I've got something to thank my dad for,' muttered Matt. 'Not that he taught me to drive for *my* sake. It was only so I could move the cars around for him on the forecourt. He'd have taught me sooner but my feet couldn't reach the pedals properly until I was twelve.'

'Matt—this is really brave of you,' Elena said, patting his shoulder slightly awkwardly.

He shrugged again. 'It's not like we can get a taxi all the way to Scotland, is it?'

'I did think about asking Mum to drive us,' said Elena. 'And

I think she might have . . . if I'd told her Tima was in trouble. But she gets nervous on motorways and anyway, she's so conked out from her pills every night, it wouldn't have been safe.'

Matt felt a pang of regret. How good would it be to have a nice, kind grown-up helping them out for a change? He liked Callie a lot. She was bright and warm and caring. She was also pretty unstable, especially when her bipolar symptoms really kicked in. Elena had to be her mother's carer when things got bad . . . but he still envied her. When they all got back from this adventure—assuming they *did* get back from this adventure—Elena's mum would hug first and ask questions later. His dad would hit first . . .

'Then, of course, she would have wanted to know how we *knew* Tima was in trouble,' went on Elena. 'And I'm not sure she's well enough to manage the truth.'

'I'm not sure *any* of our parents are well enough,' grunted Matt. 'Or ever will be.' The idea of telling Mum and Dad that he had some kind of animal-speaking superpower was just insane. They'd never believe him . . . and if he tried to prove it . . . well, his mind simply wouldn't imagine it. The part that played out little scenes of what might be was just a blank screen with the occasional zigzag.

Elena nodded. 'It slips out, though, doesn't it? The Night Speaking? I started speaking Chinese last week, when I went into the Golden Dragon for a takeaway. The *look* on the woman's face. I said I'd been watching a Chinese TV show and was just copying what I'd heard . . . but . . .' she sighed. 'I can never go back in there again . . . *Anyway*, it'll take us six hours and forty-

45

four minutes to get there, according to my satnav,' Elena went on, her face lit by the glow of her phone. 'It's a good job Tima sent us that link to check out her holiday lodge.'

Matt nodded. 'I just hope we'll be in time to . . .' he tailed off. To what? Save Tima? From what? 'Look —what do we actually know?' he said, finally.

'That she's in big trouble. And other people are too,' said Elena. 'And the danger comes from the spinning, whirling thing . . . whatever that is.'

'It's not much to go on, is it?' muttered Matt.

'No,' admitted Elena. 'But here we are in a stolen car. I guess you're feeling what I'm feeling.'

Matt didn't answer. He didn't need to. The cold dread hadn't left the pit of his belly since he'd seen Tima in the eagles' panicky minds. Elena had tentatively touched the female eagle next and got the same message as Matt; Tima, somewhere dark. And then an image of something . . . rotating very fast. And a scream. The feeling was worse than the images and the sound . . . the feeling of *dread*. They had immediately texted Tima, of course, but got no reply. They'd called too, but the call went to voicemail every time, while they cursed themselves for not telling Tima about the eagles before she'd rung off.

Elena reached across to the radio and put on a national station. 'Just in case there's news . . . of anything,' she said to Matt.

'In Scotland?' said Matt. He shook his head. 'I don't think it's happened yet.'

'Are you telling me the eagles are *clairvoyant*?' Elena spluttered.

'I don't know,' snapped Matt. He rubbed his forehead and

sighed. 'Maybe they are. I think maybe they see patterns and make predictions. It's a survival thing, isn't it?'

'I guess,' said Elena. 'Animals know stuff we don't . . . before we know it. Like, you know, tsunamis and stuff. They always run inland when there's a tsunami, way before any human knows it's coming.'

'A tsunami . . .' murmured Matt. Yeah. That's what it felt like. Whatever the hell was coming, it was coming . . . and all he and Elena could do was trust in the instincts of the animals.

They didn't really have any choice.

CHAPTER 9

'That girl . . . that girl yesterday,' said Jamie. 'She understood me!'

Uncle Fraser and Granddad looked across the table, brows furrowed, and waited for Jamie to slow down and repeat himself; maybe do a little Makaton. Some basic sign language could help them all out sometimes, when Jamie's speech really thickened up. It usually thickened up when he was excited or upset.

In his own head, Jamie sounded just like everyone else. His words flowed out perfectly fluently . . . *more* fluently than many of the kids at school. But for everyone else, apparently, it was like he was speaking through mashed potato. The words just got caught and came out muffled and misshapen. If he stuck to simple, one syllable attempts, people could often get the gist, but anything more than that needed serious effort and concentration.

Many people didn't like to hear themselves on recording devices; they got embarrassed that their voices were too high-pitched or too monotone. Jamie had no sympathy for them at all. They could at least understand what they'd *just said* when it was played back through a speaker. If anyone played Jamie's recorded words back to him (and yes, they actually had) it was garbled nonsense.

'Say it again slower,' said Granddad, spearing a slice of haggis and a rasher of bacon and wrapping a thick slice of bread around them.

Jamie took a deep breath and said: 'I—met—a—girl—yesterday.'

Granddad nodded and grinned. 'You did? Was she a looker?'

Jamie rolled his eyes. 'She—under—stood—me!'

'She understood you?' echoed Granddad.

'Aye, she did,' spoke up Uncle Fraser. 'Chatting away they were!'

'What . . . did she know Makaton?'

'No,' said Uncle Fraser, his eyebrows up high. 'It was quite something—she just seemed to get what he was saying . . . like it was a normal conversation. Maybe she has someone in her family with the same condition as Jamie.'

'She laughed at my joke!' added Jamie. 'She called me Sandpaper Boy because I said I was only safe with sandpaper . . .' He'd been thinking about that all night, mulling it over and marvelling at it. He'd replayed the conversation in his mind on a loop, trying to remember it exactly right before he spoke about it.

Of course, neither of them could make any sense of the latest sentence, because he'd been laughing as he spoke. Jamie sighed. He might get his little laptop out later and talk to them that way. He wasn't very fast at typing, because of his wonky hands and lucky dip coordination, but if he really worked at it he could get something down. He'd recently joined an online community of kids with similar problems to his and they all hugely enjoyed sharing their experiences in a closed group chatroom. The brilliant thing about words on a screen was that nobody was judging anything about you other than your grammar, punctuation, and sense of humour. And sense of humour was what they all *lived* on. You had to laugh . . .

'So . . . will you be meeting your girlfriend again?' asked Granddad, winking at him.

Jamie rolled his eyes once more and then shrugged.

'Probably not,' said Uncle Fraser. 'We were just doing a few last-minute improvements on the scenery and we're done now. But I think we can blag some tickets and watch her on stage when the show goes on after Christmas. Maybe they'll let us go backstage afterwards.'

'She's staying at Loch View,' said Jamie. 'I could walk there.'

'Slower,' said Uncle Fraser, and Jamie went into his usual auto-repeat at half speed.

'You could,' he agreed. 'How about we both walk over this morning with the dog? I still have a few things to do out there and you can help. You never know, she might be around as it's a Sunday. She might want to take a walk with Hamish.'

Jamie grinned and nodded, putting both thumbs up.

'Just don't be disappointed if she's not there,' said his uncle. 'Or if . . . if . . .'

Jamie grasped his uncle's arm and nodded heavily, tightening his smile and glancing heavenwards. 'Yeah,' he said. 'I know.'

They both nodded. Jamie had learned over time that many people could be kind. Many people would smile and make an effort. It made them feel good—decent and noble—talking to the poor *challenged* boy and treating him as if he was normal. But the feelgood didn't last. A conversation with Jamie was tiring; it demanded intense focus and effort. Most people weren't up to it for longer than ten minutes. People he'd had a pleasant chat with one day had crossed the road another day, averting their gaze or suddenly looking at their phone. Jamie tried to reason that these people weren't being unkind—they were just not up to it. He shouldn't take it personally.

But it *was* personal. Maybe he shouldn't go over to Loch View. His happy memory of the easy-going chat with that girl could be wrecked if she blanked him next time.

Only . . . he really didn't think she would. There was something about the way they had communicated. She hadn't asked him to repeat anything. She hadn't paused and wrinkled her brow, trying to understand him. She hadn't behaved as if anything about him was subnormal. Not at all. It was unlike any conversation he had ever had—even with Uncle Fraser who knew his vocal patterns and tics better than anyone.

It was as if she simply spoke *Jamie*.

They set out right after breakfast and they passed Peter Walker along the ridgeway. The light snow had eased off and the

51

sun was struggling up into the sky, picking out the purple sheen of heather on the lower slopes.

'What killed that cow of yours then, Pete?' Uncle Fraser called out.

'What's that?' replied the crofter, walking across to them with Joey, his German Shepherd. Hamish ran to greet the neighbour's dog, dropping to the ground in front of him and rolling over happily.

'Your cow,' said Uncle Fraser. 'Young Jamie here found a dead cow two days back in Brawder's Pass. We came back to take another look but it'd gone. We reckoned you'd come for it.'

Peter glanced down the glen and then back at them both, puzzled. 'I didnae find a dead cow,' he said. He wrinkled his weathered brow at Jamie. 'You *sure* it was dead, lad?'

'Aye, definitely dead,' replied Jamie. 'It had a big hole right through it.'

But Peter didn't understand a word and Uncle Fraser declined to translate for him. He placed a heavy hand on his nephew's shoulder, squeezed, and said: 'Ach, it was from some distance—he was probably mistaken. I expect it was just having a wee lie down and then got up and wandered off later.'

The crofter looked concerned. 'Aye, that's likely . . . but I *have* been missing one of my Highlands. I thought she might just have gone wandering. Joey and I are keeping an eye out.'

'Well, we'll keep an eye out too and let you know if we see her,' said Uncle Fraser. 'See you later, Pete.'

'Why didn't you tell him about the hole?!' demanded Jamie, as soon as they were out of earshot of Peter.

Uncle Fraser stopped and turned to look at him. 'Seriously, Jamie—you're the only one who saw it,' he said, at length. '*I* don't think you're making it up—but it's a pretty weird story. And you know how people can get the wrong idea about you . . .'

'Yes,' snapped Jamie. 'They think I'm not all there. They think just because I can't walk and talk properly, I've got no brain.' His words were fast and hot and he wasn't surprised when Uncle Fraser didn't reply. There wasn't much he could say anyway; they both knew the truth. Jamie grudgingly had to admit that it probably *was* for the best that his uncle hadn't mentioned the hole in the cow. The farmer and crofters they knew were all right—but some were blunt speakers and made no bones about the McCleods' bad luck, getting lumbered with a kid who would be so little help to them. Around these parts, strength, dexterity, and stamina were highly prized. You needed these qualities to survive. Jamie knew the blunt speaking highlanders were right. He *was* a liability and it was only because Uncle Fraser and Granddad loved him that they didn't ever say it.

'Best forget about it, eh, lad?' said Uncle Fraser.

'Sure,' grunted Jamie. The five lodges at Loch View were now in sight, so he made an effort to put the holey cow out of his mind. There was a chance he might see that girl again.

'Come on, Hamish,' he called, turning to see where the collie had got to. 'Come *on!*' Hamish was some distance back along the path, chasing his tail as if he was still a puppy. And he was three now! 'Come *on,*' Jamie called again.

But Hamish just kept going round and round.

CHAPTER 10

They were just south of Carlisle on the M6 when there was a bang and the Land Rover suddenly lurched left.

Elena, dozing with her head against the passenger side window, awoke with a shriek and clung on to her seat belt as they slewed sideways into the nearside lane, narrowly avoiding a lumbering cement mixer lorry. Lucky flapped wildly on Matt's headrest.

'Blow out!' yelled Matt, struggling to get the vehicle to stay left and move onto the hard shoulder. It finally obeyed and Matt thanked his lucky stars they'd only been doing about 60 mph at that point. Any faster and they might both be meat paste in a metal panini by now. His growing confidence behind the wheel deserted him abruptly as he switched off the engine, put the handbrake on, and rested his forehead against the steering wheel.

'Should've checked the tyre pressure,' he mumbled, trying to keep the shake out of his voice. Outside, the constant *vooom-vooom-vooom* reminded him that they'd broken down in the worst possible place. Motorways were horribly dangerous for a motorist in a stationary car.

'What do we do now?' gulped Elena. 'Hitch a lift?'

'Nope. Wheel change,' said Matt. He sat up and gave her a tight smile. 'It's OK. I know how.' What he didn't tell her was how incredibly dicey it was to change a wheel on a motorway hard shoulder, with traffic thundering past at 70 mph. Most people would put the blinkers on, put the tailgate up, and then get the hell away from their vehicle, up a bank or deep into a verge where they'd call the RAC or AA for rescue. Lorries were known to plough into the back of stationary vehicles, their drivers confusing the hard shoulder with a lane of moving cars.

But Matt didn't have the option of calling for help, not while driving without a licence or insurance in a stolen car. 'Lucky! Stay there!' he told the starling. She obediently stayed put on the headrest, giving her wings a disconcerted shudder. Matt got out carefully, waiting for a gap in the traffic. It was just after nine and the morning rush hour was easing off, which wasn't really a good thing. With the lanes now emptier of traffic, everything was moving faster. The only break he'd caught was that the blow out was on the passenger side, away from the road.

'What can I do to help?' asked Elena, arriving next to him as he peered at the ragged tyre. The hood of her coat was up over her fair hair and her round blue eyes were full of worry.

'I don't know yet,' he admitted. 'I've never actually changed a wheel before. I've only seen my dad do it. It's easy though.'

It *wasn't* easy. It took five minutes for them to find the tools under a panel in the boot and another ten to unscrew the spare and get it off the back. They were both crouched on the cold, gritty tarmac for another half an hour, working out how to jack the car up, get the old wheel off, and get the new wheel on. It was bitterly cold and wearing gloves made it all much harder work. Elena called up a YouTube video on her phone to be sure they were doing it right but the man in the video seemed to have no problem getting the wheel nuts off with his wrench. On their car the nuts seemed to have been welded on by an angry god of molten metal.

After nearly an hour of much sweating and even more swearing, they stood up and breathed out. The spare was on. It looked OK. They'd turned the wheel nuts as tight as they could, both of them pulling on the wrench with all their energy, grunting and huffing.

'We're good to go,' puffed Matt, finally.

But Elena shook her head. 'Wait,' she said, getting a flask out of her backpack. 'Drink this first. You're knackered. Unfit to drive.'

She was right. He was shaking with fatigue. He almost dropped the tin mug she'd filled with hot chocolate. He turned and leant his elbows against the wooden fence, which separated the motorway hard shoulder from a gentle slope down to some farmland. As he drank he watched a herd of pigs in the field below. Some were lying under tent-shaped wooden huts and some snuffling through the muddy earth outside, ears tipped forward over their big, meaty heads; they all seemed impervious to the endless rumble of traffic just a short stroll away. Elena joined him, sipping from her own mug. 'Well done,' she said. 'I would never have known what to do.'

'Yeah, you would,' he said. 'You looked it up on YouTube, didn't you? You did half the work, too.' Nobody could ever accuse Elena of slacking. 'Anyway,' he slurped the dregs of his cocoa, 'we should get off this hard shoulder. We could get splatted by a truck any moment.'

He was just dumping the tools and the wrecked tyre wheel in the back when there was a sudden short whoop and Elena gave a cry of alarm. Pulling up behind them was a traffic patrol car.

CHAPTER 11

The girl walked along the damp boulders, arms held out. She was wrapped up warmly in a silky, lightweight purple jacket, black jeans, and furry black boots, and her dark hair was tucked into a Russian style cap with earflaps. She still moved like a dancer as they wandered along the edge of the water.

'Careful!' called Jamie. 'Don't go falling in—that loch is really deep. Only a couple of steps from the shore it drops away.'

'It's OK,' she called back over her shoulder. 'I won't fall.' She sat down on a large rock and began to pet Hamish who seemed to completely adore her.

Tima had spotted Jamie and called out from the deck of her family's lodge just as they wandered past, carrying Uncle Fraser's tools. Jamie was ridiculously pleased she had remembered him. And even more pleased when she threw on her outdoor gear and came out to talk to them before letting her parents know she was off down to the lochside with her new friend. Uncle Fraser had happily shooed them off to hang out together.

'Brrrrr,' she said to Hamish. 'I should have brought my gloves. Now I'll just have to keep my hands warm in your fur!'

Jamie ambled after her and sat on a neighbouring rock with an ungainly thud. 'This is really weird,' he said.

'What's weird?' she said, playing with Hamish's ears and gazing into his eyes.

'You can understand me,' explained Jamie.

She glanced up, looking puzzled. 'What's weird about that?'

He paused, wondering if she was being serious. 'Well . . . most people *don't* understand me. I have a communication disorder. I can't talk very well. Even my uncle and my granddad have to make me slow down and repeat myself. They say it's like I'm talking in another language.'

The girl gave a low chuckle before dropping her nose to touch Hamish's. 'Ah,' she said. 'That explains a lot.'

'What?'

'Well, for a start, why your uncle was looking at me as if I'd just dropped out of a rainbow when we were chatting yesterday. And . . .' She shifted around so that she was looking directly at him, weighing him up. 'Hmmm. Well . . . I guess it would be hard for you to spill the beans to anyone else, so you might as well know . . . I'm a Night Speaker.'

'A Night Speaker? What's that?'

'Good question,' she said. 'There aren't many of us—only two others that I know; my best friends—Elena and Matt.

We all have the same . . . er . . . characteristics. One—we don't sleep very well. Two—we can communicate with animals. And three—we can understand any language on the planet—and speak it—instantly. We have abnormally large angular gyri,' she added. As if that made perfect sense. Seeing his expression she laughed, got up, and pressed her chilly fingers to the area just behind his ears on either side of his skull. 'This part of the brain,' she said, 'is where the language centres are—they're called the angular gyri. I've had an MRI scan, so I know what's going on in there. My angular gyri are way bigger than average—and there's always a crazy light display going on in there. Most people's . . . it's just a sparkler . . . but mine? And Elena's and Matt's? It's the Edinburgh Tattoo fireworks all the time.'

Jamie didn't quite know what to say to all this. He simply stared at her and then out across the loch, trying to process it. She was talking about something . . . well . . . *supernatural* . . . just like it was a talent for tennis.

He glanced back and saw she was sitting down with Hamish again. 'So . . .' he said. 'You can talk to animals too? Like . . . Doctor Doolittle?'

He expected her to laugh but she didn't. She just grinned. '*Better* than that.'

'Show me then,' said Jamie.

'OK. What do you want me to ask Hamish?'

Jamie thought for a moment. 'Ask him where I keep his dried venison.' She glanced up at him and back at the dog. 'It's his favourite treat,' he explained. 'We get venison from a deer farmer near us and we always dry a load of it to keep for Hamish to chew on.'

'It's in a basket on top of the log store next to your wood burner,' she said, smoothing Hamish between his ears as the dog gazed adoringly up at her.

Jamie felt his jaw drop. How could she *possibly*...?

'And he says he loves it but if you really want to know, his *favourite* favourite thing is actually bacon. And he's got a weird thing for satsumas too.'

'What...? I mean ... how ...?' he garbled. Hamish *did* like satsumas; Jamie always shared segments with Hamish, just to watch him take it cautiously in his teeth and then skip around crazily as the intense tang hit his doggy tongue.

'I told you—I'm a Night Speaker,' Tima said. 'Although my main thing is insects and spiders. My friends do mammals and birds more than me. Come on—let's walk a bit further. I'll have to go back soon. We start rehearsing again in Edinburgh at two.'

Dazed, he stumbled along in her wake as she moved on down the shoreline, Hamish bounding happily after her. After a while she turned, saw how far behind he was, and stopped.

'Sorry!' she said, as he caught up. 'It's a bit harder for you, isn't it? Why do you walk that way?'

Her enquiry was so straightforward it didn't occur to him to be offended. 'When I was three I was in a car accident,' he said. 'My parents were killed and I was left like this. I was normal before, apparently.'

She stood still and stared at him searchingly. 'That was bad luck,' she said, at length. 'So ... that's why you live with your uncle?'

61

'Aye—and my granddad,' said Jamie. 'I don't remember anything different. To me, I've always been . . .' he waved his wonky hands, '. . . like this.'

She nodded and then looked down into the peaty water. Its impenetrable depths were masked by the reflection of blue sky and scudding grey and white clouds above. 'Jamie,' she said. 'You know I mentioned that weird plughole thing in the loch the other night . . .?'

He nodded, suddenly feeling prickly.

'Do you think . . . I mean . . . my mum thought she felt an earthquake in the night. And this morning there's a crack in the wall in our lodge. I was wondering whether they were related . . .?'

'An earthquake?' said Jamie. 'Did she actually feel the ground shake?'

'Well, she wasn't sure whether she was dreaming or not . . .' admitted Tima. 'She comes from Yemen where they have lots of earthquakes, so she thought maybe—'

'I felt shaking too,' cut in Jamie. 'Not last night, but on Friday.'

They looked at each other for a few moments. 'Well,' said Tima, thoughtfully, 'there *are* earthquakes in the UK. We get about 200 a year. I read about it. So . . . we've maybe had a few tremors. It's probably nothing to worry about.'

Jamie bit his lip. That was the thing. He *did* feel worried. Ever since finding that cow. And he didn't normally get worried about stuff. His life was full of things that could easily worry him into an early grave if he let them—just going to school was a help yourself buffet of stressful situations but he had learned to let them wash over him, mostly. He didn't even twitch when someone called him Lurch these days.

So why had the cow and the shaking ground freaked him out so much?

'You saw something scary, didn't you?' asked Tima, stroking Hamish's ears. 'Hamish was scared too. You saw a dead thing . . .'

Jamie blinked. He'd only just got over the venison strips and the satsuma. 'We . . . we found a dead cow,' he said.

'Yes. And?' she prompted. 'There's something else.'

'It had a hole in it,' he said. 'A big, perfectly round hole . . . right through its ribs and out the other side.'

Hamish turned a tight circle and whimpered, keeping his eyes on Tima. 'It's not the hole that scared Hamish,' she said.

'It's what made it.'

CHAPTER 12

The traffic officer was friendly. 'Everything all right?' he said, as he clambered out of his car, leaving the blue light flashing on top.

'Yeah, thanks,' said Matt. 'Just had to change the wheel.'

Elena noticed he'd dropped his voice a little lower, to sound a couple of years older. She smiled at the officer—a stout, middle-aged man with a short ginger beard—and wished she looked *three* years older.

'Not easy on these four by fours, eh?' the officer said, walking right up and scrutinizing them closely. He crouched down to peer at the wheel. 'This one, is it? Nuts all done up nice and tight?'

'Yeah,' said Matt. 'Hard work but we did it. Should get us home.'

'Where's home, then?' asked the patrolman, still checking the wheel nuts and grinning up at Elena.

'Glasgow,' said Matt, without a pause. Elena blinked and smiled harder.

'You don't sound very Glaswegian,' observed the officer.

'No, I'm not. My dad moved there,' said Matt.

The officer nodded and stood up, squinting at Matt. 'You can't have been driving very long. When did you pass your test?'

'In the summer,' said Matt. 'Just after my 17th birthday. I did a lot of off road driving with my dad beforehand,' he added. It wasn't a complete lie.

The officer nodded slowly. 'Nice set of wheels your boyfriend's got,' he said to Elena.

She felt herself colouring up and stared at his ID badge—PC David Gilbert. 'He's not my . . . we're just . . .'

'We've got to get going,' said Matt. 'We're already really late.'

'So, where have you kids been then?' asked PC Gilbert, pleasantly enough, but his eyes were roaming the vehicle. Matt could guess why. A seventeen-year-old who'd just passed his test was usually driving around in an old Nissan or Ford; something small and cheap to run and insure.

'Lake District,' said Matt. 'Staying with my mum for a few days. Dad lets me borrow the Land Rover for long journeys.'

'Very nice of him,' said PC Gilbert 'Lovely part of the world, Lake District.' He turned back to Elena. 'School finish early, then?' he said.

Elena took a quick breath. 'Yes. I go to a private school,' she said, poshing up a little to sound like Tima. 'We finish earlier than state schools.'

'All right for some,' grinned the officer. He glanced back at Matt. 'Mind if I take a look at your licence, son?'

Elena felt rooted to the spot with fear. As Matt made a show of rummaging around in his pockets she managed to make herself move across to the fence where she gripped the old wooden plank to steady herself. *Breathe*, she told herself. *Just breathe. And think.*

'I might have left it in the glove compartment,' Matt was saying. She could hear the tension in his voice and hoped the patrolman couldn't.

Elena closed her eyes and took long slow breaths. *We need to get away from this guy . . . NOW.*

'Um . . . looks like I left it at home,' Matt was saying now. 'I can drop it into my local police station tomorrow if you need me to.'

'I'm sure it's all fine,' PC Gilbert was saying. 'But I'm going to have to run a quick check on your vehicle before I can let you two go on, OK?'

'Sure. Fair enough,' said Matt. 'Can we get back in and wait? It's freezing out here.'

'Your girlfriend can get back in but you hang on outside for a bit longer, all right?'

'OK,' said Matt. 'Ellie . . . get back in. We'll be going soon.'

He sounded pretty confident and she wanted to laugh— hysterically—as she got back into the passenger seat. The officer was heading back to his car to run a check on the number plate. It looked like it was all going to end here and the whole thing would be hideous; her mum wouldn't know how to cope with this. And Matt's dad . . . oh god. She didn't even want to think about what he was going to do. She wound the window down and Matt said 'Sorry.' His head was bowed in dejection.

There was a sudden loud blare of a car horn, making them both jump. Then the sound of brakes being applied. And many more car horns, beeping, blaring, and tooting. The traffic wasn't piling up in a crash but it was slowing down rapidly.

Elena felt goosebumps all over her even before she turned her head to look. Because she *knew* her little prayer had worked. They had come. They had *come*. She got out of the car and stood next to Matt, staring back down the hard shoulder in wonder. Just beyond the patrol car the fence had been broken through, splintering apart as if it was made of matchsticks.

And about twenty-five pigs were ambling along the tarmac.

The officer leapt out of his car and spun around to stare at the pigs, lifting his hands to his head in utter astonishment. A second later he snatched his radio out and began yelling into it while simultaneously waving at the traffic to slow down.

Don't go out there! Elena sent to the herd. *Stay close . . . right against the fence . . . stay safe.* The message seemed to get through because the herd—about thirty pigs now—clustered tight along the hard shoulder, close to the broken fence. Snouts were high and curly tails were twitching, but no pig was panicking.

The officer was close to panicking though. He was now bellowing into his radio. 'We've got a problem here! Pigs on the motorway! Yes—PIGS! We've got to close all three lanes NOW.'

The traffic was already slowing to a halt as he threw himself

67

behind the wheel and eased his patrol car out across the first two lanes, lights flashing. Then he got out and waved at the drivers still crawling along the outside lane, bringing them also to a halt before getting a large reflective triangle out of his boot and planting it in their path.

Now, sent Elena. She glanced to the road ahead. It was clear. They were in precisely the right place, the roadblock just behind them.

'Time to go,' said Matt.

They drove away sedately, attracting no attention whatsoever. PC Gilbert had far, far bigger problems to deal with. Through the rear windscreen Elena could see all three lanes of traffic were now stationary. A hundred or more pigs were now surging across to the central reservation barrier and planting their trotters on the tarmac. More were pouring through the broken fence and joining the others in a seething pink demo, snorting and squealing. It looked like quite a party.

Thank you, sent Elena. *Thank you so much. Give us five minutes start, OK?*

'I'll never eat a bacon sandwich again,' said Matt.

CHAPTER 13

'It's worse than the one down in Loch View.' Uncle Fraser ran his fingers along a deep crack in the mortar which had probably glued these granite rocks together two hundred years ago.

'They've got cracks down there too?' asked Agnes. Jamie had met her many times over the years. Uncle Fraser was often called up to holiday sites for his carpentry and handyman skills. He couldn't make quite enough money just crafting his beautiful furniture so he needed to do more ordinary work too. He often told Jamie he was glad of it. 'It wouldn't be good for me to spend all my time in the workshop, never meeting people, would it?' he'd say. 'And you get to come along for the ride quite often, and meeting people is good for you too.'

Jamie didn't always agree. Some people were hard work to meet; visibly recoiling from his lumpy wal coherent speaking. Others, though, like Agnes up at Glen Cawb, were great. Agnes owned and managed three holiday cottages and eight wooden lodges with spectacular mountain views, and she always had time for Jamie. When she couldn't understand him she would grab his shoulders, wink, and say: 'One more time for the awd lady with the bad ears!' And even if she didn't understand every word, she got the gist of it more often than not.

Today, though, Agnes was distracted. After a quick hello, she'd taken them straight to one of the stone cottages to show them the deep crack.

'Jamie thinks there's been an earthquake,' said Uncle Fraser, digging his long, lean fingers into the dark groove and sending out a shower of sandy grit. 'One of the lodges at Loch View has a big crack through the render. The woman staying there thinks she felt shaking in the night.'

'An *earthquake—here?*' Agnes folded her arms across her stout chest and raised her grey eyebrows.

'The UK gets about two hundred earthquakes a year!' Jamie announced remembering what Tima had told him earlier that day. They'd left Loch View behind around lunchtime to drive three miles up the glen to Agnes's place.

Agnes peered at him, wrinkling up her brow. 'Did you say . . . two hundred earthquakes?'

'Aye!' he said. 'Every year.'

'Well,' puffed Agnes. 'Of all the things . . .'

'Excuse me . . .' A young man knocked at the door. 'Agnes . . . here a la____e I can use? I can't seem to get any signal on my

'Aye, sure you can,' said Agnes. 'Go and see Barry in the office. You're the fourth person to ask me today. I think there may be a problem with the transmitter. Or maybe our WiFi booster . . .'

'Show me the other cracks,' said Uncle Fraser, when the guest had gone. 'I might be able to get some mortar up here tomorrow and mend them.'

Agnes took them off to see two other cottages with similar problems; one with a crack right along a window frame and the other with a thumb-width chasm across its stone floor. 'I've got guests arriving in these next week, staying right through Christmas,' she said. 'So if you can get up here tomorrow with your mortar and your trowel I'd be much obliged. Can't have them thinking the whole park is going to slide down the mountain!'

'Not much chance of that,' said Uncle Fraser, grinning. 'An earthquake in these parts is probably a once in five hundred years occurrence!'

Hamish was waiting patiently for them in the back of the Jeep, his ears silhouetted against the grey sky as early dusk descended on the mountains. It was only just past mid-afternoon but the light faded fast on December days like this. 'Come on,' said Uncle Fraser, starting the engine and giving Agnes a wave. 'Let's get home and have some of your granddad's soup.'

More sleet was falling as they bumped up the track across Agnes's land. Jamie grabbed the strap above the passenger door, hanging on it instinctively as the thick off-road tyres negotiated rocks, ruts, and hard-packed snow. In a few minutes they reached the smooth surface of the main road—itself not much more than a single lane—and were able to pick up speed.

Uncle Fraser broke the easy silence. 'So . . . will you be meeting up with Tima again?'

Jamie could hear the tease in his voice and chose to ignore it. He shrugged. 'Maybe.' He didn't say that he and Tima had swapped mobile numbers. He'd told her that he only ever used text on his phone, because people *really* couldn't understand a word when they couldn't even see his face and his pantomime hands. He didn't text often either, because it wasn't easy for him to do. He'd been given the phone when he'd turned twelve last year, for emergency purposes rather than SnapChatting his mates. One—he didn't really have the mates for it, and two—he didn't really have the thumbs for it.

The signal was very random around the mountains too, but he always kept it charged and in his pocket and it had been useful a few times. It also made him feel like he belonged to the 21st century.

'Stay in touch,' Tima had said. 'I won't be around much but we could go out with Hamish again sometime, maybe. And . . . this thing with the cow. If anything else strange happens, tell me, OK?' There had been a seriousness about her when she'd said this. She wasn't just curious—she was concerned; as if she knew something he didn't.

'She said we might go out again with Hamish,' he finally added—speaking slowly —knowing his uncle would be pleased.

'That's great,' said Uncle Fraser, wrenching the car into

third gear and speeding up along the road as it climbed over a high ridge. 'She's a really nice WHOA! WHOA! HANG ON! HANG ON!'

A stag had leapt right across the Jeep. Its woolly hide and wild eye were suddenly flying through Jamie's field of vision and there was a sharp clunk; a hoof striking the bonnet. Uncle Fraser jammed on the brakes and then let them go again as the car started to skid towards the ditch at the side of the road. All around them were deer. Panicked, stampeding deer. It was a miracle there wasn't a crash. Uncle Fraser wrestled with the wheel and the gear stick and brought the Jeep to a juddering halt. They sat, open mouthed, while twenty or thirty of the wild animals plunged past down the mountainside. Even through the panicked barking of Hamish in the back, Jamie could hear the thundering of their hoofs on the road.

'What the hell?' croaked his uncle.

'Something spooked them,' Jamie said; the words a tangle even to his own ears. The sense of dread that had stalked him ever since he'd found the holey cow suddenly leapt into his belly, twisting him up inside.

Uncle Fraser undid his seatbelt and got out of the car. Jamie followed and they stood for a moment, watching the last of the deer disappear down the mountainside. Then they both turned and looked up the slope. The ridge above them looked perfectly normal, except ... except for some dark drift of ... what? Smoke? Jamie fleetingly wondered if the benign mountain had s***ly become a volcano.

'*** that?' asked his uncle. 'Is someone setting a

campfire up there?'

Jamie shook his head. No mountain trekker in their right mind would set up camp so high on such an exposed ridge of rock.

'Stay in the Jeep,' said Uncle Fraser. 'I'm just going to check it out. Could be a fallen climber trying to attract attention. C'mon, Hamish, let's see what you can sniff out.'

'Wait—let me come too!' protested Jamie. Hamish seemed less keen. His ears were flattened back and he was whining.

'It's all right, boy,' said Uncle Fraser, opening the door and coaxing the collie out. 'The deer have gone now. It's just you and me . . . and maybe someone with a bust leg!' He had ignored Jamie's protest altogether.

Jamie got back into the passenger seat, jangled and annoyed. He knew he wasn't the best climber in the world but he could manage a gentle slope like *this!* And it was a lot scarier sitting here on his own than it would be following his uncle and Hamish. He leant onto the dash and peered up through the windscreen. Yes—further up on the ridge there was still a thin wisp of smoke drifting in wind-snagged ribbons. Uncle was probably right. It was most likely an anxious walker who'd got caught out by the sudden gloom descending, setting up a fire to keep warm and attract attention. Tourists were always heading off unprepared and having to be rescued . . . although not so much at this time of year. Most tourists who came in December had a 'snow in' fixation, fancying log fires in a luxury lodge with a picturesque blizzard raging outside. The reality was some different, especially when the WiFi failed and then t out of wine and couldn't immediately get to Waitrose—but the holiday cottage owners had the sense not to mention this in their brochures. They made good money out of Christmas.

Jamie took a long deep breath and let it out again as slowly as he could. There was nothing to worry about. Any moment now Uncle Fraser and Hamish would be back, along with a limping, embarrassed tourist.

But why would an embarrassed tourist set off a stampede like that? Those deer had been *afraid*. Really *afraid*. He could see it in the way they'd moved and the rolling of their eyes, picked out in the headlights. The deer were used to people walking about; they would move away but they wouldn't be afraid. Unless someone was trying to shoot them. Could that be it?

Panic seized him afresh. What if it *wasn't* an embarrassed tourist? What if it was some deranged stalker with a rifle? He got out of the car, scanning for the man and dog. He needed to go after them and warn them. He slammed the door shut and began to run up the slope, stumbling through clumps of heather and low, winter-blackened gorse, his heart thudding hard beneath his thick coat.

Sleet stung his cheeks and melted away in the heat of his breath as he climbed the steep, increasingly rocky fell. 'Uncle!' he yelled. 'Come back!' He didn't know which route they'd taken— to the left of the rocky outcrop above or to the right? His eye had been on the sky. A sudden flare of white light pulled hi to the right. Smoke or steam was rising from this point to clambered on, breathing heavily, the air carving a thin, chi path down his throat and into his lungs. He reached the c the ridge, dropped into the shallow basin on the other side—and saw two impossible things.

One: a deer, in two pieces.

Two: A huge, spinning, steaming, gleaming set of perfectly circular jaws, retreating into the mountainside behind a plume of steam.

Jamie fell to his knees, shock knocking the air out of him. He made some kind of noise—a wail or a scream—he wasn't sure. The front end of the deer was close enough for him to reach out and touch, its tongue lolling and its dark eyes blank and staring right at him. Its top end was separated from the bottom end by perhaps a metre. The wound that had sliced it in two was, on both sides, a perfect, smooth curve. A smell of charred meat drifted with the steam.

But all of this was a sideshow, gathered in a blink. Jamie's eyes were now riveted on the spinning silver jaws as they pulled back into the sloping wall of rock. A grinding, sliding sound came from them, with a bass note like a low, rumbling scream.

Then someone swore in his ear and he found himself smashed face-first into the ground. There was a thud, as if the air had been sucked away and then fired back again, and Jamie slid into unconsciousness.

CHAPTER 14

In the early afternoon, Elena called a halt.

'You're nearly asleep. You just drifted across two lanes,' she said. 'We have to stop. We have to get some rest.'

Matt wanted to argue. His intense worry about Tima and whatever the eagles had been trying to tell them had not left him since the early hours of that morning. He still didn't know what that danger was . . . but he knew exactly what kind of danger he was putting Elena in if he kept trying to drive on so little sleep. He pulled off the motorway at the next services. He parked the Land Rover at the furthest reach of the car park well away from the shopping and dining area.

'Try Tima's phone again,' he said, rubbing his face.

Elena did but the result was just the same. It went straight to voicemail. She'd already left three messages begging Tima to call them right away. There was no point in leaving another. 'They're in the mountains,' Elena said. 'Signal is always dodgy in places like that. Or she could be in rehearsals in Edinburgh and just not picking up.'

'What about this place where she's staying? Loch View?' said Matt. 'They must have a landline number we can call.' They got the number from the holiday site's web page and called it but nobody picked up. Matt's anxiety didn't ease off.

'Look,' said Elena, flicking screens across her phone, 'if anything BIG has happened up in the Highlands, it would be all over social media and the BBC website by now, wouldn't it? And there's nothing. Apart from pigs on the M6, of course.' She gave a little grin, flashing him some driver's mobile phone footage of pigs running joyfully around all three carriageways earlier that day. Traffic had been held up for nearly an hour, apparently, before all the pigs were safely back in their field. 'So, whatever it is, it hasn't happened yet,' Elena went on. 'And even if it has . . . we can't do anything in this state. We *have* to sleep. Try to get a few hours now and then we can go on. OK?'

Matt couldn't argue. His head was spinning with exhaustion. His own small phone lay in his pocket, dead. He could switch it on at any time but he knew the deluge of anxious messages he would find on it would make him feel worse still. And what if all this was for nothing? What if Tima was fine? What if the eagles were just . . . messing with his mind?

Why, though? Why would a pair of golden eagles fly hundreds of miles to play some inter-species prank on him? No. The animal world had never lied to him in all these months since he'd become a Night Speaker. Something was definitely wrong. And he clearly wasn't going to find out what until he rested his brain for a few hours.

They agreed he would take the back seat and lie down properly, under the tartan travel rug. 'I'm fine in the front,' said Elena. 'You need sleep way more than I do. Lie down properly.'

She fed Lucky a few dried mealworms from Matt's stash in his backpack. Then she let her out of the window, to get in some fresh air and stretch her wings. The starling flew a few turns of the car park and then roosted in a branch of a cedar tree, which hung over the car. Elena closed her eyes and let herself drift.

She was awoken by a clunking sound and looked up into the furry grey face of a squirrel. Spread-eagled across the windscreen, it had obviously just jumped down from the branches overhead. Elena got up, glancing back at Matt. He was sound asleep, buried under the car blanket. Lucky, still in the branches overhead, was watching the squirrel, apparently unconcerned. Elena realized she'd slept for quite a while. It was beginning to get dark. No other cars were parked nearby. She pressed the window control button and the glass slid down quietly, allowing a cold December breeze to buffet her face. She stretched her hand outside and the squirrel immediately leapt onto it and climbed up to her shoulder.

'Do you have something to tell me?' she asked, keeping her voice low. The squirrel jumped onto her lap and turned three tight circles.

'Yes . . . we know about the circles,' she told it. 'We just don't know what they *mean*.'

The squirrel looked at her. It didn't seem to be able to offer much more.

'OK—yes or no answers,' said Elena. 'Is Tima in danger?'

Yes.

'Is she still in Scotland . . . in the mountains?'

Yes.

'Can we help her when we find her?'

The creature seemed uncertain; this made her insides scrunch up in panic. Maybe they were already too late . . .

'Just . . . give me an idea of the kind of danger she's in!' she pleaded.

The squirrel turned three tight circles again and then leapt up above the steering wheel and began to drum its feet. It made such a rumble across the grey plastic moulding that Matt shot up from under the blanket, grunting: *'What?'*

The squirrel continued to drum until a van suddenly pulled up to the right of their car. Then it shot back out of the window and up into the branches of the cedar and was gone.

Matt climbed back into the driver's seat and stared across at Elena. 'What the hell was that about?' he asked, grabbing a bottle of water and taking a gulp.

Elena sighed. 'More circles. And rumbling. And Tima *is* in trouble and she is in the mountains . . . but it couldn't tell us whether we could help.'

'Well, someone must think we can help,' said Matt. 'Or else why are all these animals going to the trouble of contacting us?

It's bigger than just Tima being in trouble. It's got to be.' He started up the engine. 'So let's go.'

CHAPTER 15

If anyone could babble, Jamie could. His words tumbled, squawking and crazy, out of his unhelpful mouth. He sounded like a fight in a henhouse. He made about as much sense too.

'Jamie! Jamie, STOP!'

Uncle Fraser looked wild-eyed with worry. Jamie knew he'd been found and carried back to the Jeep; he had a dim recollection of being laid down on the back seat and strapped in, Hamish whining and licking at his face, a throbbing pain on the side of his head. Then he must have faded out again because the next thing he remembered was being carried into the house and Granddad shouting out 'Fraser! Fraser, what's up wi' the lad?'

Then he must have slept again and now here was a man he only vaguely knew, pressing something cold to his chest. Ah. It was Doctor Calman, listening to his heart. The chilly stethoscope woke him up and he immediately began to shout warnings to his uncle. And they made, of course, no sense at all.

'Maybe I should give him a sedative,' said the doctor and Jamie immediately shut himself up. He did not want to be sedated. He needed to talk about what he'd seen.

'It's OK,' he said, slowly and deliberately. 'I'm all right. I just . . . hurt my head.'

'Jamie, sit up gently,' said the doctor, 'and look at my pen.' He held up a silver ballpoint and began to move it slowly from side to side. 'How is your eyesight? Have you got any double vision?' Jamie shook his head, which throbbed at the left temple in response. He felt it and discovered a padded dressing had been stuck to it.

'Can you see normally?' went on the doctor. Jamie glanced around. He was on the old leather sofa near the open fire. It was dark outside and the clock on the mantelpiece was at twenty past six. How long had he been out of it? 'I can see fine,' he said, nodding heavily to be clear.

'Do you feel sick?' asked the doctor.

Jamie shook his head. 'No,' he said. 'I feel hungry.' He rubbed his stomach.

'Ach, well that's a good sign!' said Granddad.

'Are you dizzy?' asked Dr Calman, putting the pen back in his pocket and getting another gadget from his bag.

'No . . . I'm OK,' insisted Jamie. He realized that talking about what he'd seen needed to wait until it was only his uncle and grandfather. Uncle Fraser must have seen it too—he obviously didn't want to discuss it in front of the doctor.

'Good—now keep your eyes wide open.' The doctor shone a bright light into each of his eyes in turn. Then he checked his ears. 'All looks fine,' he said.

'Do you think we should take him to A&E?' asked Uncle Fraser. 'Should we have gone right there?'

'No, no—I think you'd still be waiting to get seen if you had,' said Dr Calman. 'It's been a very heavy weekend in Stirling, with all the Christmas build up. You did better calling me in; I'm just sorry it took me so long to get here. But, he's been awake on and off, yes?

'Aye,' said Uncle Fraser. 'But sleepy. And, as you can see, he took a dent to the skull when he fell over.'

'I think he's going to be fine,' said the doctor. 'It's all cleaned up now and it didn't bleed much. Just a belter of a bruise, I think. The skull is pretty robust when you're thirteen. Keep a close eye on him for the next day or two and if he starts being sick or getting dizzy or a bad headache, call me right away—or 999 if you can't reach me. All right, young man?' He turned back to smile, briskly, at his patient. 'No running around on mountains in the gloaming again, OK?'

Jamie grinned weakly and nodded.

They saw the doctor off and Granddad went to heat up some soup on the stove while Uncle Fraser sat down next to him. 'So then, Jamie. What happened? Why did you come running up the mountain like some crazy bampot and bash your head on the rocks?'

Jamie blinked. '*What?* Didn't you see the deer? And the *thing*—the spinning thing—in the rock.'

'Again. Slower,' said his uncle.

Jamie took a deep breath and concentrated all his energy on his speech. He needed to stop babbling and be slow, steady, and clear. 'I got worried. I thought there might be a crazy guy up there with a gun.'

'A crazy guy . . . with a gun?' checked Uncle Fraser. 'Why would you think that?'

'I don't know—and it doesn't matter!' went on Jamie, speeding up in his impatience and then having to take another breath and slow down again. 'When I got there—to where the smoke was coming from—I saw a deer. It was CUT IN HALF.'

'Wait—hold up!' Uncle Fraser held up his hands. 'Did you just say you saw a deer . . . cut in half?'

'YES!' cried Jamie. 'It was cut in half—like the cow was tunnelled through. The cuts were curved too, and smooth, like in the cow. Like it had been tunnelled through too . . . but it was smaller so it just broke in half.' He knew he sounded crazy. His uncle was still trying to fathom what he'd just said; then he turned and got a notepad and pen—something he always had to hand for the times when his nephew just got too excitable to understand.

'Draw it,' he said.

Jamie grabbed the pen and paper and did a quick sketch of the dead deer in two pieces, cut through with perfect curves. Then—for reference—he drew the holey cow too, with arrows from one to the other, pointing out the similarity of their fatal injuries.

Uncle Fraser leaned across, watching, and then took the

notebook and stared at it. 'Jamie . . . is this really what you saw?' he asked, in a low voice, glancing across into the kitchen where Granddad was buttering bread to go with the soup.

'Yes! AND I saw what did it!' Jamie snatched back the notebook and drew the massive, terrifying circular jaws. What he sketched was also perfectly circular with row upon row of jagged metallic teeth, spinning and whirring in different directions. He even drew the wafts of steam it had been giving off.

'It's . . . amazing,' said Uncle Fraser. Jamie did not like the tone of his voice.

'*That's* what killed the deer,' said Jamie, banging his fist on the drawing. 'And the cow.'

Uncle Fraser took the notebook again and looked at the drawing for a long time. Then he sighed and put the notebook on the coffee table.

'You *see?*' insisted Jamie. 'You see how that thing made the hole? How it broke the deer in half? It explains everything! It just came right out through the rock and killed them.'

His uncle steepled his hands together, and leant his chin on them, letting out a tired sigh. 'Jamie,' he said. 'Hamish and I came and found you. You were lying face down on the ground with a bleeding head. But there was no deer. And no hole in the rock. And no . . . animal killing machine. Just a boy who'd fallen over and knocked himself out.'

Jamie gaped. *What?*

'Look . . . I think you must have got a bit spooked, come up after me and then tripped and concussed yourself. And that must have given you some kind of weird dream or . . . or

8 6

hallucination.'

Jamie felt as if he'd been kicked in the chest. 'But . . .' he began. 'But . . . I didn't trip! I was hit—pushed! And look . . . the cow. I wasn't spooked or concussed when I saw *that*, was I?'

His uncle shrugged. 'I don't know . . . and, seriously, right now I'm too tired to make sense of any of this fantastic story.'

'You think I'm making it up?' snapped Jamie, suddenly furious.

'No!' His uncle rubbed his eyes. 'No . . . I don't think you'd do that. I just . . .'

'What . . . do you think I'm going soft in the head?' Jamie whirred his fingers angrily at his temple.

Granddad put the soup and bread and butter on the table. 'Whatever you two are arguing about, stop it right now!' he warned. 'You're not to say another word until you've had some soup and bread. You too,' he said to his son. 'Come on. Get to it and then Jamie is going to bed.'

Jamie realized he was ravenously hungry. He pushed down the anger and picked up the soup. If he hadn't already decided what to do next, he would have been too upset to eat—but he'd just remembered that he had Tima's number. And she had definitely said: 'This thing with the cow. If anything else happens, tell me, OK?'

She believed him. She knew it was true because Hamish had backed him up. So . . . as soon as he could, he was going to text her and tell her everything. Half an hour later he was in bed, texting in the dark. But the message wouldn't send. It kept pinging back at him with a little exclamation mark in the corner. Jamie re-sent and re-sent and re-sent. He even crept out to the hallway and right up to the front door where the most reliable signal was always to be found—but nothing. Just the exclamation mark. He wanted to kick the door, he was so frustrated.

A furry body pressed against the back of his legs. Hamish. The dog stared up at him and whined.

'*You* know something's wrong, don't you?' murmured Jamie, keeping his voice low. Uncle Fraser and Granddad were in the sitting room talking together. A sudden idea struck him. For Hamish the journey to Loch View, straight across the glen, would take only minutes. The dog could run like lightning and he was good with directions. Jamie knew Tima's scent would be on the bit of paper she'd written her number on; after a sniff of the paper Hamish would understand where he was meant to go.

Jamie crept back to his room and got out his notebook and pen.

CHAPTER 16

Tima had gone to bed early. The rehearsals that afternoon had been intense and as much as she was loving it, while Mum was driving her back to Loch View she was already falling asleep.

Mum and Dad had just about kept her awake, asking her about the rehearsal as they'd eaten dinner. After a while, though, they noticed her answers were getting shorter and shorter. Then Mum had said: 'Darling girl, you look like you're about to fall asleep in your plate! Why don't you get an early night?'

Tima nodded. 'I will.'

In bed she had checked her phone out of force of habit. There were no calls or messages. She quickly texted Matt and Elena just to say hi—but found the message wouldn't send. There was obviously some issue with the WiFi here. Of course, the Highlands were notoriously patchy when it came to mobile phone signals—there were hundreds of mountains in the way—but the holiday lodges were meant to be connected to really good WiFi. Not right now, they weren't.

She sighed, too tired to worry about it, switched the phone off and went to sleep.

Scratch.

Scratch-scratch-scratch.

Tima shot up in bed, realizing the noise she could hear was not just inside her own head. Blearily she prodded the bedside clock and it lit up blue to inform her that it was seventeen minutes past eight. She'd only been asleep for an hour.

SCRATCH.

She sprang out of bed and ran to the window, drawing back the curtains. At first she saw only condensation and then a black nose squashed against the glass, making her jump. Another scratch and she realized who was out there. Lit softly by the strings of fairy lights around the lodge park, a border collie was up at the window, paws on the stone sill, panting.

'*Hamish?!* What are *you* doing here?' she murmured. Something tickled against her hand and she looked down to see a small zebra spider running around in tight circles across her knuckles. She dropped it on the sill and grabbed her thick fleecy robe from the back of the door. Stuffing her feet into her slippers, she crept past the closed door to the cinema room, where Mum and Dad were watching a movie, and went outside.

The dog was waiting for her on the frosty decking. It looked directly into her eyes and then turned a tight circle before sitting down and whining softly.

'*Sshhhh!*' hissed Tima, glancing back to the lodge. 'What is it? Is something up with Jamie?'

The picture the dog sent into her head was confusing and panicky. Jamie was in there somewhere . . . lying face down on grass. And frightened deer were leaping through the air. But there was something easier to read. Literally. A rolled-up piece of paper was stuck in the dog's collar. Tima tugged it out and unrolled the message.

TIMA! I have seen what killed the cow! It killed a deer too! Under this line was a drawing of what looked lik£EEEEEEEe circles of teeth . . . with curved arrows indicating spinning movement. Tima had a flashback to the spider turning circles on her hand a few minutes ago and shivered. The note went on:

Uncle F thinks I hit my head and dreamt it but it's REAL! V scared. - Jamie

Her heart began to speed up in an oh-so-familiar way. She took Hamish back to her room, telling him in no uncertain terms to stay completely silent; he did. Once there she tried to text Jamie but again, it wouldn't work. Obviously Jamie hadn't been able to get a text out to her either or he wouldn't have needed to send Hamish. Did this phone cell black out have anything to do with the other weird stuff going on around here?

Tima took a deep breath. It was time to be old-school practical. So . . . she grabbed a notebook and pen and wrote her own message back:

We need to meet. Send Hamish again around midnight, when my mum and dad are asleep, so he can take me back to your place. Can't text you—phone signal's gone. -Tima

She tucked the message into Hamish's collar, explained it thoroughly to the dog too, to be on the safe side, and sent him home. Half an hour later the dog was back, panting, at her window, with another message.

In the middle of the night? Are you crazy? If you don't mean it just send Hamish back and I'll try to see you tomorrow. If you ARE crazy, keep Hamish with you and I will meet you halfway, just above the Ballachry Waterfall at midnight. Hamish can take you the safe way if you ask him. Bring a torch!
- Jamie

CHAPTER 17

'I don't believe it.'

Matt got back into the driver's seat and shook his head.
The queue ahead of them—red tail lights glowing—snaked on
and around a bend in the valley. They were maybe an hour away
from Loch View, where Tima was staying, but they were going
nowhere. Mountains rose on either side of them but it was too
dark to see anything other than the foothills, illuminated by the
traffic jam.

'What is it?' asked Elena. 'What's the hold up?'

'I don't know but nobody's going anywhere.' Matt raked
his hands through his thick dark hair and blew out his lips in
frustration. 'Put the radio on . . . see if you can find anything out.'

Elena tried but couldn't raise anything other than hiss and
static on the in-car radio. After another ten minutes Lucky

began to get stressed, flapping around on the back seat. 'Let's pull the car over to the verge,' said Elena, 'in case any emergency vehicles need to go past. And then we can get out, walk up, and see what's happening.'

They weren't the only ones with this idea. Loads of cars were parked with two wheels across the crushed snowy grass at the edge of the road. Happily the snow they'd encountered a few miles back had eased off a while ago but it was still cold. A hundred headlights lit their way as they picked a path along the verge. As they walked they heard murmurs from others who'd made their own voyage of curiosity and were now heading back. 'They're going to cut through the barrier,' said one man, stopping at the window of a stationary van.

'What's happened?' asked Elena.

'Just get around the bend and see for yourself,' the man replied. 'Don't want to spoil the surprise.'

They broke into a run, Lucky flying just above their heads, and as they came around the bend the blue and red flashing light show of five police cars lit up a bizarre scene. A huge metal monolith lay on its side, upended across the steep valley. Covered with discs and antennae, it made Matt think of a toppled Martian invader.

'It's a transmitter mast,' he said, gaping. 'The whole thing's come down from the hillside. How the hell did *that* happen?'

'It's like the Highlands don't *want* us to get to Tima,' murmured Elena, shivering.

'Well at least it explains why we can't get a phone signal,' said Matt.

'But . . . it looks like it's only just happened!' said Elena.

'It's the third one to go down today,' said a woman nearby, wrapped up in a duffel coat and woolly hat. 'I reckon it's terrorists.'

Matt and Elena headed back to the car as two fire engines went past, presumably to cut a way through the metal barrier between the lanes of the A road, allowing the trapped traffic to do a U-turn and head away from the blockage.

'How are we going to go on?' asked Elena, back in the passenger seat. 'I can't even get my sat nav working now!'

'We find a garage and buy a map,' said Matt. 'There has to be another way around.'

It took an hour just to crawl along the carriageway and do a U-turn through the broken metal barrier and another half an hour before they reached a small filling station and shop at the edge of a wooded valley. Matt was getting seriously concerned about money as they queued to buy the road map book of Scotland. He only had a tenner and a handful of loose change left in his pocket. He was getting seriously hungry too and he knew Elena must be starving—they'd finished up their food supplies hours ago—but they might need all their money for petrol. There was only a quarter of a tank left in the Land Rover. This journey should have taken six hours—and they'd now been travelling for well over twice that.

The man ahead of them in the queue wasn't helping Matt's mood. He was complaining loudly about a coffee machine, which had apparently failed to deliver what he wanted.

'I paid for a LARGE cappuccino and *this* is what I get!'

The man, wearing a suit and a Rolex watch the size of a teacup, slammed his drink down on the counter, slopping a good third of it across the surface. 'You people can't even be bothered to fill the machine up correctly, can you?'

Matt felt his teeth clench. *You people.* He'd heard that said to his mother, when someone decided to have a go at her for being Polish and living in England. The young Asian guy on the till reminded him of Ahmed at school.

'Sorry, sir,' the young man said, remaining civil even though he must want to slap the customer *so* badly. 'The machine is probably running out. We've had a lot of people in thanks to the road being blocked.'

'I don't want your excuses. What are you going to do about it?' demanded the man.

At this point another man, older, arrived behind the counter. 'What's the problem, son?' he said, flicking a glance at the growing queue.

'The coffee machine is broken. I need to give this man a refund,' said the young man.

For some reason this simple exchange seemed to incense the customer. 'Oh, I see how it is!' he suddenly started yelling. 'Just start jabbering away in your own language to make the customer feel small!'

Matt couldn't help it. He tapped the man on the shoulder and said: 'Look mate, cool it, yeah? We're all tired. All he was saying is that the coffee machine's bust and you're getting your money back.'

The man swung around, staring furiously into Matt's face.

'Oh! Oh really? And you'd know that, would you? You speak fluent bongo-bongo do you?'

Matt narrowed his eyes. 'As it happens, yes. Only it's Punjabi.'

The men at the till, alarmed, were now back in English. 'Please sir,' said the older man. 'I am happy to give you a full refund.'

'No, no—wait!' crowed Rolex Man. 'This youth thinks he speaks your language. Go on—prove it! Speak their language! Let's all celebrate the multicultural!'

Matt smiled and then turned to the bewildered-looking men behind the counter. 'I'm sorry you have to deal with planks like this,' he said, enjoying the astonishment on their faces . . . and the falling jaw of Rolex Man . . . as he slipped easily into Punjabi. 'If you like I can arrange to have his stupid face pecked off by crows.'

'He's not even joking,' said Elena, joining in and getting a gasp of bafflement from Rolex Man. 'And we're too tired to care what's right or wrong any more, so I might send a plague of rats up his trousers too.'

The garage employees began to hoot with laughter—and other people in the queue started to join in. It was unlikely any of them understood a word but they were clearly fascinated and entertained by watching two polite teenagers showing up a badly-behaved adult.

'Here is your money, sir,' said the younger man, handing over some coins. 'Was there anything else?'

The man didn't reply. He just snatched the cash, left the drink on the counter, and stormed out of the shop. Matt and Elena bought the map book, sharing grins with the staff.

'It is most unusual to meet young white people who speak Punjabi,' said the older man, beaming at them. 'How did you come to learn it?'

'Gap year,' lied Matt, with a shrug. 'We spent it working our way around India.'

Out on the forecourt they saw Rolex Man hadn't yet left. He was standing up next to the open door of his Audi, parked just a few steps from their stolen Land Rover, holding up his phone and swearing at it. Matt guessed he wasn't getting any cell coverage either. On the dashboard lay something leather and gleaming. Matt, getting back into the driver's seat, had barely even formed the thought before there was a blur of feathers and suddenly the man was bawling even louder.

'My wallet! My bloody wallet! That bird just stole my wallet!'

Matt and Elena got out again and stared up in shock as a dark feathered form swooped across the forecourt and vanished into the trees. Elena stared at him across the bonnet, her eyes wide. *'Lucky?!'* she mouthed. Matt nodded, biting his lip.

Rolex Man was now chasing across the forecourt, staring into the inky darkness of the wood that hemmed it, and yelling in fury.

'Couldn't have happened to a nicer bloke,' said Matt, getting into the car and opening the sunroof. They'd driven a few metres down the road before the wallet landed on the back seat, closely followed by Lucky.

'You *thief!*' admonished Elena, laughing.

They pulled over five minutes later at a small roadside diner and discovered the man was called Ryan Snell, was a wealth management consultant, and had £230 in cash in the wallet. There was an assortment of credit cards too. 'We can send the wallet back to him in . . . Canary Wharf,' said Elena, staring at the address on his business card.

'Yeah, if we feel like it,' said Matt, extracting the notes.

'Matt—of course we must!' said Elena. 'And . . . this . . . it's not our money.'

'No,' he said. 'It's Lucky's. She found it. And you don't mind us spending it, do you Lucky?'

'Don't mind,' said Lucky.

'But it doesn't seem right,' insisted Elena. 'We're not thieves. I don't care how rude he was—I don't like stealing from him.'

'Call it a loan then,' said Matt, with a sigh. 'We've got his address; we'll just borrow some and send it all back in a couple of days. He'll manage.'

Elena still looked guilty.

'Seriously—you are *so* goody-goody,' said Matt. He rubbed his weary face. 'Listen to me. We *need* to sit down, eat a hot dinner, and make a plan—you know we do. Who do you care about more? Rolex Man or Tima?'

CHAPTER 18

Jamie felt like he was in some kind of fairy story as he watched Tima approaching down the track to Ballachry Waterfall, led by Hamish. She looked like the girl in *The Snow Queen*, in her fake fur hat and gloves and expensive boots.

He stood, wrapped up in his thick winter coat and finally found words. 'I can't believe we're really out here at midnight!'

'Midnight is a bit early for me,' said Tima, flashing her torch towards his face. 'I usually get up an hour or two later. Hey—what happened to your head?'

He patted the small dressing on his left temple. 'Oh—I was hit. Fell on my face and must have connected with a rock.'

'Who hit you?' she asked. 'Or *what*?'

'I think it was some guy,' he said. 'I heard him swearing . . . in another language, but you could tell. Then—wham!'

'But where were you? No—don't explain now. Let's walk and talk.' She patted Hamish's neck. 'He really wants to take us back to the scene of the crime. Is it far?'

'Not too far,' said Jamie. 'And not too hard to climb as long as the snow holds off.'

He told her everything he could remember as they made their way up the valley behind Hamish. A bright three-quarter moon was up which helped them greatly; Tima's skinny torch beam could only dance around in the immediate area and pick out troublesome rocks, holes, or knots of heather. Even so, Jamie fell over three times.

'Are you sure you're OK?' she asked on the third time. 'I mean . . . you might be concussed still.'

'Tima,' he said. 'One, it's dark—and two, I'm *me*. There's a reason why they call me Lurch at school.'

She chuckled sympathetically. 'You don't lurch,' she said. 'But it *is* quite a funny name.'

'Could be worse,' he said. In spite of the cold pit of fear in his belly, he felt warmed through by the pleasure of talking to someone so easily. He had literally never had such free-flowing conversation.

'So—the stampede that drove you off the road,' she said, puffing a little and reaching forward to grab at tussocks of heather as the climb got steeper. 'Do you think the whole herd was freaked out by the same thing you saw?'

'It looked that way,' said Jamie, remembering the wild eyes and the thundering hoofs. He was working hard to keep up with Tima, who was as fit and lithe as any wildcat. Concentrating on keeping his unruly limbs on task was at least distracting him from the fear of what they might find beyond the ridge.

'Is that it?' asked Tima as Hamish suddenly bounded ahead, towards the slanting summit. Thin fingers of frozen snow reached down from the flattened peak, tapering out into shadowy heather, rock, and scree. The collie reached an outcrop, gleaming white in the moonlight, and paused, looking back at them, flattening his tail. Jamie didn't need Night Speaker powers to read that Hamish was scared. As scared as *he* was.

They reached the spot a few seconds later. He recognized the way the ground dipped in a shallow basin, the shelter of the rock stopping the steady, cold push of the wind. Jamie stood and stared around. There was nothing here. Hamish turned a circle and then sat down on the grass with a thump.

'It was here!' Jamie said, his voice shrill with frustration. 'Right here!'

He dropped his face into his palms and muttered: 'Unless Uncle Fraser was right and I *did* just hit my head and dream the whole thing!'

Tima was kneeling next to Hamish, shining her torch down at the wiry grass and clumps of heather. 'Nope,' she said, poking at the ground. 'I don't think *that* happened.' She lifted her fingers and sniffed them. 'Yup. That's blood. But the body has gone . . . just like the body of the cow disappeared. Someone came along and removed it.' She stood and went to the wall of rock, running her hands over it. 'This is harder to explain.' Jamie had to agree. The rock looked completely solid. There wasn't even a crack in it.

'But . . .' went on Tima, 'something has been disturbed here.

The insects that live here . . . they've all gone.' She closed her eyes. 'Yes . . . just around here. It's . . . empty.'

Jamie couldn't work out what insects you could ever find on a lump of rock around here. *He'd* never seen any.

'They're tiny,' said Tima, as if she was reading *his* mind now. 'Mites and ticks and midge larvae. You'd need a magnifying glass and a torch to see them. I only know that they're *not* here because . . . well, I just know it.'

Hamish gave a throaty whine and stood up. He looked as aggravated as Jamie felt.

'He knows something weird is going on,' said Tima. 'He didn't see what you saw . . . but he's picking stuff up. He's . . . wait . . . someone's coming.'

They both swung around as a tall, dark figure loomed up over the edge of their little basin in the rock. Jamie caught his breath. Silhouetted in the moonlight stood a stag, watching them.

'Well . . . hello . . .' murmured Tima. 'Have you come to help?'

The stag stepped down towards them, steam pluming from its wide black nostrils. It didn't seem in any way afraid, although Hamish would normally have sent a whole herd of deer running. Today the pair of them seemed to be *communicating*. The dog stood still, its eyes fixed on the stag's. The stag leant down until its nose touched Hamish's. Then it lifted its head, turned, angled its antlers downward, and ran right for the rock face. Tima only just jumped out of its way in time. 'Stop it!' she yelled, as it cracked against the surface. 'You'll hurt yourself.'

But the stag did not stop. It backed up and then ran at the rock again, head lowered, antlers primed. It struck hard, its strong shoulders jarring.

And then the rock . . . collapsed.

The stag pulled back, shaking its head and sending fragments of stone flying.

Jamie stared, amazed. There was a gaping hole in the rock and through it—if he wasn't going completely mad—a light was shining.

CHAPTER 19

The light was a warm golden colour. Tima moved closer, knelt down, and examined the hole, running her fingers carefully along its edge. The rock abruptly crumbled away to reveal a perfect circle. Jamie dropped down next to her, staring into it. *'See?'* he said.

She nodded. 'I do see.'

Beyond the perfect hole was a perfect tunnel, about as high as her shoulder as she knelt. The rock face had obviously just been a thin scab of granite. 'It's like . . . like the work of a trapdoor spider,' she murmured.

Jamie glanced at her anxiously.

'I don't mean it's been *made* by a massive spider,' she said, patting his shoulder. 'Just that a trapdoor spider does the same thing. It makes a tunnel and then it builds a thin trapdoor of earth and silk and pulls it across. But it has threads of silk reaching outside past it and when a fly or a beetle walks over the threads it flings the trapdoor open, drags its dinner in, and slams the trapdoor shut.' Jamie shuddered visibly. 'It's *brilliant*,' Tima insisted. 'Unless you're the dinner.' She glanced around, feeling slightly foolish, for strands of silk—and saw none. 'Whatever made this tunnel also made a thin covering, to disguise the hole it had made. That's pretty clever.'

'What I saw yesterday didn't look pretty clever,' said Jamie. 'It looked pretty terrifying.'

'OK,' said Tima. 'Describe it to me again.'

'I didn't see it very clearly,' he said. 'But it was round with lots of teeth, moving in circles . . . some clockwise and some anticlockwise. It was . . . I don't know . . . like a machine . . . but *not* a machine. There was . . . steam, I think . . . like it was breathing.'

'Did it make a noise?'

'Yes . . . I think so . . . steaming and grinding,' he said. 'But there was a lot of noise in my head when I saw it. Panic noise from seeing the dead deer. So I can't be sure.' Jamie looked up at the stag, which was standing some way off, gazing down at them both. '*He* might be able to give you more.'

'Not really,' said Tima. 'He's as scared as you were. He saw his friend die. But what I can make out from him seems to be the same—something spinning and shining and scary.'

'So . . . what are we going to do?' Jamie ran one hand around the curved edge of the tunnel and bit his lip.

'Do?' Tima blinked at him. 'Well . . . we're going in of course!'

'You want to crawl *in there?*'

'Well . . . it's not that I *want* to,' said Tima. 'Just that I don't think we'll find out much more until we do.' She looked up at the stag. 'Can you hear anything in this tunnel?' she asked. 'Or sense it?'

The stag lowered and tilted its head as it focused. Then it looked up at her and gave a little shake of its antlers.

'Hamish?' she checked. The dog gave a head tilt, listening hard, and then lay down and looked up at her calmly. 'Good,' said Tima. 'There's nothing close by. Look—we don't have to go crawling in for miles,' she said to Jamie. 'Just a little way in to take a better look. I'll go first.'

'No!' protested Jamie. 'It's dangerous, let me go first!'

She squeezed his arm and said to Hamish: 'Stay here. And if we're not back when the sun comes up . . . go for help. OK?' Hamish settled down with a low whine and the stag turned and left as quietly as it had arrived. 'Come on,' said Tima.

Just inside was a perfect funnel of rock, which widened until they were able to stand up easily, with a metre of headroom. The ground under her boots was mostly flat but the walls and ceiling were arched and smooth. The golden glow was some way distant, throwing a dim light across Jamie's anxious face as he climbed awkwardly through the hole behind her. She shone her torch to examine the rock more closely. It wasn't just black and grey as she had expected; it was patterned in long, rippling streaks of colour ranging from salmon pink to deep maroon. In the light sheen of the perfectly cut curve, it was quite beautiful.

'Look at this!' she marvelled, as Jamie caught up with her,

puffing and agitated.

'You should let me go first!' he muttered. 'I'm older! And I'm a boy!'

'Hmmm. Ageist *and* sexist,' she said. 'Is that normal for the Highlands?'

He scowled at her and she softened. 'It's very noble of you,' she said. 'But I'm fine. And honestly—something might just as easily come at us from behind as up front. Anyway—look at this!' She directed the thin torch beam across the arc of stone above them.

'Aye, it's jasper,' said Jamie, unimpressed. 'They sell it in the tourist shops.'

'Jasper?' she repeated. 'It's beautiful. Is that what these mountains are made of?'

'They're mostly granite,' said Jamie. 'But they have seams of other rock and minerals. There's lots of jasper in these parts. You can get green marble over on the islands, sapphire on Harris . . . and quartz and amethyst and even gold across other parts of Scotland.'

'Wow,' she said. 'I never knew.'

Jamie rolled his eyes. 'I think there's something here a bit more *wow* than all this,' he muttered.

'Yes . . . come on,' she said and moved on down the tunnel. They'd travelled in a slight curve, so when she glanced back past Jamie, she could no longer see the distant dark circle of night where they'd come in. It made her insides screw up a little. How far inside the mountain had they travelled? And how far down? Because the tunnel was definitely sloping.

She halted, listening intently. No. Nothing. No noise apart from Jamie's slightly laboured breathing. No insects or spiders to ask, of course, because this was not a natural passage. Maybe only hours ago this precise spot had been solid rock. Now it was air. She took a long slow breath, noting that she *could* breathe. She'd heard of people suffocating in mines when there was a build-up of gas. If Matt had been here he'd have been watching Lucky carefully to see that she was OK. Birds and other animals reacted to bad gases more quickly than humans. Maybe she should have asked Hamish to come in with them after all . . .

'Why have you stopped?' whispered Jamie. His muffled words blatted back off the rock, flat and dry.

'Just checking the air quality. Can you breathe OK?'

He took a few ragged breaths and nodded. 'I think so. Can you smell gas or something?'

'No,' she said. 'Not gas. But . . . something.' Of course, all this rock had recently been carved right through—that had to leave a smell. It was an intense mineral scent she was picking up but also something else she could not identify. 'We're feeling OK, though,' she said. 'So . . . let's push on a bit further. See what's round the bend.'

What was round the bend took her breath away. The golden light was coming from a massive natural chamber. Tima stood rooted to the spot, staring up and around, dimly aware of Jamie crying out in amazement as he rounded the curve. She had been in a cave earlier in the year but it was *nothing* compared to this. The huge domed ceiling was as high as a house and the chamber itself was roughly circular and big enough to fit three or four houses into. Unlike the tunnels, this cave looked natural with randomly undulating walls and many shadowy folds of rock and conical formations in its ceiling. The soft golden light radiated from a single papery pod hanging like a giant wasps' nest from a stubby stalactite high above their heads. The whole chamber made Tima think of a London underground station ... minus the trains and the tracks and all the people. Although now that she looked at it, the floor *did* have tracks. There were shallow grooves running along the rock floor, criss-crossing between the tunnels.

She wandered further into the cave, pulling off her hat and gloves as she stared around; it was quite warm in here.

'Where do all these tunnels go?' said Jamie, also taking off his hat and gloves.

'Maybe the mountains are full of them,' said Tima, her voice now carrying in the large space. She cast her sixth sense around instinctively, seeking insects and spiders. There were a few here, up above them in the dark folds. Cave spiders and mites mostly; too far away to get a conversation going.

'What's that?' said Jamie. There was a pile of rock in the centre of the cave. It rose up to about shoulder height. Something was sticking up out of it.

'It's ... a leg,' said Tima. Her nose twitched. That other smell she'd been picking up. She was beginning to suspect they'd found the source of it.

Jamie said: 'Don't follow me.' He pinched his nose and walked to the far side of the rubble pile. Tima watched his face pucker with disgust and sadness. 'It's the deer,' he said. 'Or ...

most of it. And . . .' He covered his mouth and nose with both hands and hunkered down to peer inside the rock. 'It's the cow too,' he said.

Tima circled the rocks, holding her nose. Jamie was right. The carcasses were stiff and cold but the smell was still pretty bad.

'It's like someone buried them,' said Jamie, puzzled. 'Or tried to.'

There were no insects on the dead animals. Nothing to communicate with. 'Come on,' she said, with a shudder. 'Let's look around a bit more.'

They headed for the tunnel to their left. 'Wait!' Tima turned, ran back, and dropped one of her gloves by the mouth of the passage they'd just arrived through. 'So we remember the way out,' she said, nudging it behind a ridge of stone. Then she followed Jamie.

The next tunnel was an exact replica of the one they'd just been in, but the patterns of pink and red were interrupted with seams of yellow here and there. 'That's jasper too,' Jamie said, when she paused to run her fingers across it. 'You get it in red *and* yellow.'

They wandered on. Their path was sloping slightly upwards and curving to the right. The air still seemed fine, but Tima couldn't guess how far this tunnel went. Maybe they should do the sensible thing and turn around now. Go back to the mountainside; go down to Jamie's place and get his uncle to come up and see all this. Just because she was a Night Speaker, it didn't mean that she wasn't allowed to ask an adult for help.

It was Jamie who'd started all this, after all. She *could* actually just leave it to Jamie and his uncle to get the investigation going. She could go back home, maybe get another hour's sleep before breakfast ... head off to rehearsals as usual.

Then it started.

It began at her feet; almost ticklish through the thick soles of her walking boots. She turned and stared at Jamie, catching the spark of fear in his eyes just as the first needle prick of panic arrived in her belly. The tickle became a vibration and then an audible rumble. Its source was not ahead of them but behind them.

'It's one of those things!' gasped Jamie, his face a mask of terror. 'It's coming this way!'

Tima grabbed his hand and ran deeper into the tunnel, cursing herself for being so stupid. They had both gone up a blind alley with no idea where it went. Now whatever had made this tunnel was coming along it. Coming right after them! And what would it do when it saw them? Pause and politely back up? The unwelcome image of the cow and the deer flashed through her mind; this tunnelling entity was not in the habit of stopping. Why would it need to? It could pulverize *rock!* A living animal ... a human being ... would be like a lump of butter in its path.

The tunnel began to ring and thrum and a warm pulse of air buffeted Tima's hair across her face as she twisted to look back in horror at what was coming to kill them. The golden light was gone, replaced by a white round glow in the centre of a mass of moving parts. Just as Jamie had said, it was a huge set of spinning jaws, turning smoothly in rings of clockwise and anti-clockwise teeth. Towards the centre, just below the white light, the smaller rings protruded in a cone shape. There was something almost beautiful—mesmerizing—about the instrument of doom bearing down upon them.

Tima felt her knees begin to buckle beneath her as panic melted them. There was no way out. No way out this time. Her Night Speaker powers counted for nothing here, deep in the bowels of a Scottish mountain. All the astonishing things she could do made no difference. She was about to die, and worse, Jamie was about to die with her and it was all her fault.

The spinning jaws were only a few metres away; she could feel the steamy warmth of all those whirring, working, relentless parts.

'I'm so sorry, Jamie,' she sobbed. 'I'm so sorry.'

CHAPTER 20

'I'm going to phone Mum,' said Elena, as they finished their fish and chips. Now that she was full of food it was easier to think straight and she knew she couldn't put her mum through any more worry. She had to call. It was stupidly late but the diner was full of motorists who'd been stuck on the road for hours thanks to the fallen transmitter; it didn't look like they were going to close and turn down all that business any time soon.

She flipped open her phone and read the messages she'd got earlier that day, before they'd got as far as Scotland, when the mobile coverage was still OK.

Got your note. Not worrying, I promise. But who is the friend and where have you gone? I need to tell the school something. xx

Elena hated lying to Mum. She avoided it whenever

possible because Mum trusted her; relied on her. It was almost, sometimes, as if Elena was the parent. Because Mum was often out of it on the pills she needed to take, her sense of time passing could drift—which could be helpful sometimes . . .

It was now hours since Elena had last texted. That morning, while Matt was still driving them towards their breakdown, she had responded: **Please tell the school I'm with you today. Tell them I'm fluey or something. I'm OK—I'm with Matt. We're worried about Tima and we've gone to talk to her. Will let you know when I'm on my way back. Love you. xxx**

And her mum had sent back: **OK. Will do. Please call me soon, though, or I will worry. xxx**

Elena sighed and rubbed her face. Even if Mum had been having a dozy day and had not noticed time passing for a while, she surely would have begun to worry by now. 'I'm going to ask to borrow the landline,' she said, getting up.

Matt nodded. 'Just . . . don't say where we are,' he said. 'Don't give too much away. And . . .' He looked awkward. ' . . . maybe, ask her to call my . . . no. Forget it.'

'She can call your mum! It's OK,' Elena said.

'It's not OK,' he muttered. 'If she does then my dad will know you're with me. And when I get back and there's trouble . . . you'll get in trouble too. Just . . . don't worry about it.'

Elena sighed and nodded. She saw his point but she felt bad for him. It wasn't fair that all the fallout from their mad adventure would only land on him.

In the end, after she'd given the manager of the diner a quid (*he said the phone was getting used non-stop because of the cell outage in the area and he had to charge*), there was no need to handle Mum's questions . . . because Mum didn't pick up. She was probably asleep by now. So Elena left a message on the answerphone: 'Mum—I'm so sorry not to call sooner. I'm up country and there's something wrong with the mobile phone network around here, so I'm calling from a landline. Look—I'm fine. I'm safe. I'm with Matt and we'll find Tima tomorrow and sort out our . . . problem. Can you, please, just not worry? I promise this is all for a good reason. I will try to explain when I get home. Love you . . .'

She hung up, feeling both bad and relieved. It would have been lovely to hear Mum's voice amid all this freakiness. But it would also have been really hard to explain what was going on. Because the truth was . . . she didn't *know* what was going on. Neither did Matt. All they knew was that weird stuff was happening in the Scottish Highlands and Tima was right in the middle of it. And in serious danger from . . . *something*.

That sounded pretty lame even to her . . . even with golden eagles and grey squirrels giving them warnings and the fallen transmitter lying across their path like a harbinger of doom.

She closed her eyes and thought about the beam. It would be travelling through her room in . . . she checked her watch . . . seven minutes. She wished she could be there to feel it; to hold on, for a few seconds, to its wonderful, calm, uplifting song. It might take the terrible, spinning fear out of her chest.

CHAPTER 21

Tima no longer knew anything. Not even who she was. Her end was coming and all she could hope, as her legs gave way beneath her, was that it would be quick.

A hopeless glance behind revealed the bringer of her death, right on her shoulder, spinning and glittering and devoid of compassion. She braced for the impact of the jaws.

Then she was yanked violently sideways.

It took her a few seconds to understand that she was still alive. Someone was breathing heavily in her face; someone shaking and gulping. Tima blinked and then held her ears as the rock worm—for this is what it had become in her mind—moved on past with its ear-splitting hiss, whine, and rumble. She only accepted that her death had really been postponed when the noise began to fade and the golden light began to filter back across Jamie's wide, scared eyes.

She gaped in bafflement at her saviour. Jamie was hunched up against the wall of this tiny alcove.

'How . . . how did you find this?' she burbled, her voice high and thin with shock.

'Don't know,' he breathed. 'I just saw it in the corner of my eye as we ran.'

'Wow. Fast reflexes!' marvelled Tima, her heart finally slowing down just slightly from its jackhammer pace. 'You just saved my life!'

Jamie turned around, barely blinking at her thanks, and ran his hands around the alcove. It was no more than a couple of metres deep and curved like the inside of a ladle; the ceiling skimmed their hair. It looked too perfect to be a natural cave. 'It's a dead end,' said Jamie, patting the rock. 'Because . . . look . . . there's only granite here. Maybe that thing only wants to eat the jasper. It had a taste of granite, didn't like it, backed up, and changed direction.'

'Do you think it's *eating* rock?' said Tima. 'Or just cutting through it? Mining it? And what *is* it? Some kind of rock worm . . .? It's a machine—but it—it has *presence*. There's something *animal* about it too. I could sense it.'

'It's a mining grub. Part machine—part animal.'

Tima jumped violently and they both spun round to see a silhouette blocking the exit from their life-saving alcove. The man was not much taller than Jamie, but stocky and muscular. Tima couldn't see his face but got an impression of fur and leather and a sweaty stink.

'Who are *you*?' demanded Jamie, following Tima out of the alcove.

'What did he say?' asked the man. He had a gravelly voice with an accent she couldn't quite place.

'He wants to know who you are,' she said, gulping. 'So do I. And I want to know what you're doing with that . . . rock worm thing . . .'

'Mining grub,' repeated the man. 'It's mining minerals.'

'And killing animals!' added Jamie.

'What did he say? He doesn't sound right,' said the man. 'Is he wrong in the head?'

'No,' snapped Tima. 'He's more right in the head than anyone I know.'

The man shrugged. As Tima's eyes adapted she could pick out a wide, round nose and small eyes inside a lot of furry beard and hair. With the whole mining thing going on, she couldn't help thinking of mythological dwarves . . . except he was of normal size.

'Who *are* you?' Tima asked again.

The man just sighed. 'I thought he'd be trouble,' he said. 'I tried to steer him away.'

'What—by knocking me out?!' asked Jamie, steadying himself against the rock and glaring.

'What did he say . . . ? Oh—forget it,' the man said. He rolled his eyes. 'I tried to help by knocking him out so his people would take him away and then not believe him. I got the cow and the deer inside and sealed the breaches. But I see it didn't work.' He shook his head. 'Now what am I supposed to do with you?'

'Just let us go,' said Tima, keeping her voice low and sweet. 'We're sorry we messed with your mining. I'm sure it's all fine . . . you've got permission and filled in all the forms, yes?' She heard the desperate edge to her voice. Was there any chance at all this miner was going to play along?

The miner snorted and then laughed. 'Yeah—that's right. All the forms were filled in.' His laugh went up and up in pitch until he sounded certifiably insane. Then it stopped, suddenly. 'Animals get killed all the time,' he said, softly. 'Industry kills animals. Not deliberately. It just happens. Sometimes the grubs go too fast and breach the surface with their probes. And if something is out there and doesn't move away quickly enough . . .'

'What planet are you from?' asked Tima. She didn't mean it sarcastically. There was no doubt in her mind that she was addressing an alien. She could hear it in his voice, for one thing—and for another, there was no way a cyborg rock-eating worm was standard equipment in British mines.

He stared back at her but didn't answer her question. He just gave a low whistle and somewhere in the distance, a rumble began.

'What's that? What are you doing?' Tima heard the panic in her voice. Calm. She must keep calm.

'I can't let you go,' said the miner, shoving them both back into the alcove. 'Not now you've seen the grubs. You'll tell.'

'We won't!' said Tima, struggling against him. 'I promise we won't!'

'*He* won't,' said the miner, pointing a stubby finger at Jamie. 'Or, if he does, nobody will understand him or believe him—but you. You look a bit too sharp. How do you know I'm . . . not from here?'

Tima closed her eyes briefly. *Why had she said that?* 'I didn't know . . . I don't,' she said. 'It's just a figure of speech!'

The miner stared at her, unconvinced. The rumbling grew louder.

'It's coming back!' yelled Jamie, clutching her arm. 'He's bringing it back! It's going to get us!'

'Don't do this!' begged Tima. 'Don't kill us! You know it's wrong. I know you do . . .'

But the rumbling got louder and louder and the man still stood there, running a grey tongue along his lower lip and staring at her through narrowed eyes. She leapt at him, trying to fight her way past; Jamie did the same—but the miner was almost as solid as the rock around them. He just thrust them backwards with his huge, meaty hands, as the rumbling, whirring, and steaming got louder. The light from the grub's single white eye suddenly flared across the tunnel behind him. Then it twisted around until it was glaring right at them, an arm's length from the miner's back. The miner stepped aside, out of its path. He gave another whistle.

And the mining grub spun its kaleidoscope jaws.

CHAPTER 22

For the second time in minutes, death was coming for Jamie. The whirring, steaming, grinding metal jaws were upon him. And Tima. The last thing he would ever feel—apart from gut-churning terror—was guilt for getting her involved. She did not deserve to die like this.

He flung himself in front of her . . . as if that would help. Then he closed his eyes and waited for the end.

The whirring and grinding abruptly stopped. The steaming went on a little. The end did not come. Jamie eased one eye open and saw the bright white glare of the grub just a hand's width from his face. It seemed to have stopped. The steaming was easing down and soon there was no noise apart from the ragged breathing of a pair of kids trapped in a tiny air pocket in the granite. The white light dimmed a little.

'It's . . . it's stopped,' he mumbled.

Tima eased around him and approached the now motionless face—if that's what you could call it—of the mining grub. 'It's doing as it's told,' she said, carefully putting her fingers onto its eyelight. 'I don't think he intended us to die. He just wants us to stay put.' She gazed around their rock prison. 'We're trapped.'

'HEY!' yelled Jamie. 'Let us OUT!'

The only response was the sound of the miner's heavy-booted feet trudging away down the tunnel.

'How long for?' murmured Jamie, sinking to the ground, suddenly exhausted. He glanced at his watch. It was just past 3 a.m. In a few hours it would be getting light. Would Hamish go and get help from Uncle Fraser and Granddad? He hoped, desperately, that the collie wouldn't decide to follow them into the tunnel. He couldn't bear to think of Hamish meeting a mining grub. Hopefully Tima's instructions in fluent dog would mean Hamish would do exactly as she'd asked and run home for help at dawn.

Tima was resting her forehead against the white light in the centre of the jaws. 'That's not safe,' observed Jamie. 'It might start up again.'

'No,' she said. 'It's not going to.'

'How do you *know*?' he asked. 'It could decide to finish the job at any moment! Or that miner bloke might decide he can't ever let us go and it would be easier to mash us up.'

'He might,' said Tima. 'But this creature won't do it of its own accord. It doesn't want to.'

'Are you . . . *talking* to it?' Jamie gaped up at her.

'Kind of,' said Tima. 'It's part animal. And I can talk to animals.'

'OK . . .' Jamie was doubtful. He'd got his head around the astonishment that she could communicate with Hamish and with that stag . . . but with some kind of alien cyborg *rock eating worm* . . . ? 'What is it saying?'

Tima sighed. 'It doesn't want to kill us. It doesn't want to kill anything. It's not carnivorous.'

'But it seemed like it *meant* to kill us a few seconds ago.'

'Seemed,' said Tima. 'But it was only blocking us in— because it was told to. It's not very happy about that either.'

'So maybe it can *un*block us!' said Jamie, hope flaring in his chest.

'Maybe,' sighed Tima. 'But the robotic part of it is programmed to obey the miner. I don't think the animal part of it can resist. In fact . . . I think *it's* as trapped as we are.'

'So . . . that's it, then,' said Jamie, slumping back against the wall. 'We're all trapped and there's nothing we can do.'

'I wouldn't say that,' said Tima. She reached up and collected something small and dark from a finger-width gap between the stationary grub and the top of their cavern. Sitting down next to him, she allowed the thing to run across her hand. It was a spider, no bigger than a five pence coin. It had a shiny bulbous abdomen of dark brown and orange. Its legs were tapered to fine points and had brown and orange stripes. 'She's a cave spider,' said Tima, her voice soft as the creature nestled into her palm.

'How do you know it's a she?' he asked, staring at it.

'I just *know*,' said Tima. 'But if you don't speak spider, you can tell by the palps . . . the tiny feeler-like things on either side of her jaws. Male spiders have fatter palps, like little boxing gloves; the female's palps are much thinner.'

'OK,' he said. He didn't know what else to add. They had a spider for company. Whoop-de-doo.

'Can you pass on a message?' Tima asked the spider. 'To anything that travels outside this cave? To a fly, maybe? If you can let it go . . . ?'

Jamie made a noise which was half laugh, half sob. After everything they'd just been through, it was hard to accept that Tima was really turning to a spider for help. She didn't say anything else, but gazed at the spider for another minute. The spider gazed back at her. It moved its palps occasionally but otherwise it sat quite still in her palm. Were they *talking* in some way? Was Tima a spider psychic too?

Eventually she stood up, gently cupped her palm high against the wall, and let the spider go. It ran up to the crack and out of sight.

'So that's it? That's the plan?' Jamie couldn't help sounding sarcastic.

'Have you got a better one?' asked Tima.

CHAPTER 23

The alternative route to Loch View was a B road full of twists, turns, and hairpin bends, winding up and down through the mountains.

'We need more fuel first,' said Matt, pulling in at another 24-hour service station a short distance from the turning Elena was picking out on the map with her torch.

He filled the tank and felt a guiltless pleasure at spending £60 of Rolex Man's cash on fuel. Elena looked a little stricken, though. 'I'm going to post that wallet back tomorrow,' she muttered.

Queuing to pay, Matt spotted a display of tightly-packed sleeping bags and grabbed a couple while Elena picked up more food and water. It seemed like this journey through the night might never end; they might as well be prepared. On an impulse he also bought a coil of fine, strong towing rope.

Most of the traffic seemed to be heading back down to Stirling on the A road. They turned north-west again on the narrow mountain route and soon found themselves high in the peaks with no other motorist in sight.

Elena peered at the map with her torch and muttered: 'We could be there in an hour if we're lucky. It's difficult to tell, though, on these roads. They really wind about and . . .' She tailed off just as Matt took a sharp breath and slowed right down, gripping the wheel hard.

'What was that?' whispered Elena.

Matt was now moving the car along at walking pace, all his senses on alert.

'It was a kind of . . . rumble . . .' he said. 'The car sort of . . . vibrated.'

'Could it have been a gust of wind?'

Matt hoped so but it really hadn't felt like it. On the back of his seat he felt his feathered friend thrumming with anxiety. 'What is it, Lucky?' he asked. 'Do you know something we don't?'

'Don't,' echoed Lucky.

'Don't what?'

A fresh blast of sleet hit the windscreen, flaring in the headlamps. 'Whoa!' called out Elena, and Matt braked just in time to avoid driving into a stag. The beast stood like a statue, antlers high, right in the middle of the road.

Matt switched the engine off, his heart thudding hard in his chest. 'Could it be a stampede . . . that rumbling?'

Elena shook her head. 'No. It's only him. Wait . . .'

She unbelted and climbed out of the car. Matt followed, glancing back to check for approaching headlights, but the road behind was all blackness. He noticed there was a rough track off to the right, leading into a flattish, stony area with a tall pile of logs to one side.

Elena was already nose to nose with the stag, which was breathing steam all over her face. 'We have to get off the road and stay here a while,' said Elena, reaching up and stroking its furry cheek. 'At least until dawn. He says it's not safe to carry on just yet.'

'OK—there's a track just over here. Let's go there,' said Matt.

They got back in the car and he drove it down the track, parking just beyond the stack of logs but not too close; he didn't want to risk the whole pile avalanching onto them. And as another of those weird rumbles made the car shake, he knew it was a good decision.

'It's OK,' said Elena, winding down her window to connect with the stag which had followed them in. 'We won't move again until it's light. Thank you.'

'Does he know where we're going?' asked Matt.

'I think so,' said Elena. 'And I think he knows why too. But he won't let us move now . . . not until it's light. So . . . come on. Let's sleep.'

Matt gave her a hard stare. 'It's at least three hours before dawn. Since when did we sleep at this hour?'

Elena shrugged. 'We're a long way from Thornleigh . . .'

maybe we can. Break out the sleeping bags!'

They got into the new bedding which was surprisingly warm. Zipping himself in, Matt was very glad he'd spent Rolex Man's cash on something so vital. Elena had taken the back seat this time and he reclined as far as he could in front while Lucky roosted on the headrest. Outside the stag cropped some grass as it blocked their way back to the road. It would have been quite relaxing if it hadn't been for the occasional, inexplicable rumbling beneath the mountain.

'Do they have volcanoes in the Scottish Highlands?' he muttered.

'They never used to,' said Elena, from the back seat. 'But these days I can believe just about anything ...'

CHAPTER 24

Exhaustion hit Tima and Jamie after the spider left. There was nothing to do now. Shouting for the miner didn't work. Talking to the mining grub didn't work, although Tima did wonder, once or twice, whether it *would* move for them if she found the right way to ask. But it was alien; very alien. All she could really sense from the animal inside the robotic outer skeleton, was that it did as it was told, like it or not. It was bred to do as it was told. It *existed* to do whatever it was told.

Eventually she sank down next to Jamie and they both drifted into a fitful sleep. Until the shaking started.

Tima shot upright in a panic, thinking at first that the grub might be starting up and moving in to pulp them after all. But the grub was in the same place, motionless, its light dimmed as if it was powered down to standby. And the shaking was beneath them . . . around them . . . in the very *rock*.

'This is what happened when I saw the cow!' cried Jamie, also up on his feet and pressing his hands to the wall behind him.

'And what Mum felt in the night,' breathed Tima, her heart pounding hard again as the shaking beneath her feet rolled on. 'It's an *earthquake!* How many is that? At least three in three days! That's not normal for this country. It can't be.'

Jamie stared across at the grub. 'Is it *you?*' he asked. 'Are there more of you? Are you making tunnels all through the mountains until they collapse?'

The grub gave no response but Tima was nodding. 'That's it. That's got to be it. We have no idea how many of these things are here, under the mountain. There could be dozens . . . hundreds. And if they're all chomping through the rock and leaving tunnels everywhere . . .'

The shaking subsided but there seemed to be a high-pitched buzz of stress in the very air around them. Tima closed her eyes, bringing back the image of the large cave chamber they'd first wandered into. All those tracks across it from one tunnel to the next; it was easily big enough for many mining grubs to pass through it. But what had happened to all the rock the creatures had pulverized in their terrifying jaws? It couldn't just go into their massive, worm-like bellies and vanish, could it? That wasn't physically possible. There should be . . . droppings. Piles of rocky grub poo.

'What are you *doing* with all the rock?' she asked the grub. 'Where is it going?'

In response the eye suddenly lit up, half blinding her, and the grub gave an unearthly whine. Its shining teeth began to spin. Tima yelped in fright and threw herself back against the wall where Jamie was cowering, his hands over his eyes.

A sudden movement of air made her realize that the grub wasn't coming towards them; it was backing away, curving itself around the lip of their tiny cell and reversing up the tunnel. It stopped after a few metres, letting out a low sigh of steam before falling silent again. Tima peered out of their small cavern and right into the face of the miner. She considered shoving past him and running and then rejected the idea. *She* might get away, but Jamie wouldn't. Jamie couldn't sprint the way she could— and she wouldn't leave him behind.

'How many of these things are you running?' asked Tima, pointing at the grub.

The miner didn't respond. He dumped a large brown bag, made from some kind of rough woven fabric, on the floor and pulled a battered metal flask from it and something wrapped in pale cloth. He sat down cross-legged and spread the cloth, revealing apple-sized lumps of brown stuff, which could have been bread or meatballs or potatoes. It was hard to tell.

'You might as well have something,' said the miner. 'You're not going anywhere.'

Tima glanced at Jamie and they both sat down opposite the man. At least, whatever else he had in mind, he didn't seem to want them dead, thought Tima. He pulled two equally battered metal cups out of the bag, poured water out of the flask into each of them, and passed them over.

'Thanks,' said Jamie, taking his with one shaking hand. The other—his left—seemed to have seized up into a claw; it twitched from time to time, held tight against his chest. Tima could see that stress and exhaustion were affecting Jamie's movements; he drank the water and the left side of his mouth let some of it go in a stream down his chin.

'Are you OK?' she asked, squeezing his arm.

Jamie nodded. 'I just get . . . a bit knotted up . . . when I'm . . . scared,' he said.

'Tell him to eat too,' said the miner. 'You'll be a long time hungry if you don't.'

Tima picked up the round brown thing—it was heavier than it looked. 'What is this?' she asked.

'It's a meat-bread,' he said. 'It's good. If you don't want it I'll eat it myself.'

Jamie took the meat-bread, sniffed it, and then bit into it. 'S'OK,' he said, after a few bites. 'Like a heavy Marmite doughnut.'

Tima bit into hers and found it surprisingly easy to consume the thing in a matter of seconds; she realized she was ravenously hungry. She washed it down with the water, which tasted faintly sooty.

'Are you going to tell us what you're doing here?' she asked. 'If you're not going to kill us, you might as well.'

'I might kill you,' said the miner, chewing noisily on his meat-bread. 'Haven't decided.'

Tima gulped and tried to stay cool. 'You won't kill us. You're not a murderer.'

'How do *you* know?' he said. 'I'm a wanted man. There's big money on my head,' he added, with pride.

'So . . . how did you get all these mining grubs down here?' asked Tima. 'Without anyone noticing?'

He grinned. 'You guessed right. I *am* from another planet. We came in on a corridor from just outside your galaxy.'

'Through a corridor?' Tima had heard of such corridors before but she thought better of letting him know.

'You people would call it a wormhole,' said the miner. 'But it's not wormy. Or a hole. It's a corridor. You can only make one if you know how and I . . .' he grinned through a mouthful of meat-bread and tapped his nose. ' . . . I know how.'

'What's your name?' asked Jamie.

'What did he say?' the miner said, wrinkling his face in confusion.

'He wants to know what your name is,' said Tima. 'He's Jamie and I'm Tima.' She hoped if he knew their names he might be a bit less inclined to kill them.

'Vardof,' he said.

'So . . . is this your job?' she asked. 'Mining with grubs?'

He gave a cackle. 'No. I'm a traveller. A merchant. A—'

'—pirate?' suggested Tima.

He pursed his lips, shaking his head. 'Freelancer,' he corrected. 'Adventurer. Risk-taker. Buyer, seller, trader . . .'

'Oh. We thought you were a miner,' said Tima, glancing at the grub, which was back on standby mode behind them. Further down the tunnel she could see a similar light and guessed another grub was guarding the exit.

'I am today,' he said. 'But when I've got all I need I will be a trader again. And I'll make a fortune.' He grinned, chewing noisily. 'I found this mining freighter . . . just floating through space. Full of grubs and nowhere to go. So I took it.'

'What happened to the crew?' asked Tima.

'Mostly dead,' he said, cheerfully, taking a swig from the flask. (Tima made a mental note not to have a top up.) 'Caught some space virus.'

'*Mostly* dead? What about the living ones?' Tima asked.

'Carrying the virus. Had to be quarantined,' said Vardof.

'Quarantined? Where did you put them?' she pressed.

'Oh, you know . . . outside,' he said.

'Outside *in space?*' Tima gulped. Her assumption that this man was not a murderer was taking a battering.

'Best thing for them,' he said, grabbing another meat-bread. 'They were suffering. It was a kindness.'

Tima pictured the sick crew drifting off into the vacuum of space, struggling to breathe; feeling their blood boil; imploding. She shivered. As if in sympathy, the rock around them trembled again for a few seconds.

'These earthquakes,' she said. 'We think maybe it's your grubs that are causing them.'

'All planets have earthquakes. It's natural,' said Vardof, stoutly. He wrapped up the remaining meat-breads and shoved them back in the bag.

'It's not natural around here. This is *not* an earthquake zone,' said Tima. 'What are you doing to protect the mountains you're mining through? How many grubs are out there making tunnels? And what are you doing with all the rock?'

'Taking it back through the corridor, of course,' said Vardof. 'I've made tunnels for miles—all the way back to the portal cave. When they're full up I take the grubs back to it and wham them through to the other side. They dump their loads and I bring 'em back through again. I'm on a remote Cornelian moon. Nobody bothers me. Got my cleftonique key from a Targan dealer and connected my own corridor.' He beamed at her, clearly very proud of his scheme.

'So . . . have you mined before?' asked Tima.

'I told you—I'm an adventurer. An opportunist,' he gave off another worryingly high-pitched laugh. 'I pick things up fast, make my money, then drop 'em again.'

'So . . . you don't know anything about mining,' concluded Tima.

'I don't *need* to know,' said Vardof. 'The grubs know. I just had to learn how to set them off, tell 'em what I wanted, then stop them, bring them back, and unload them. Which is what I'm doing.'

There was another rumble beneath them and Vardof was jolted sideways as he gathered up the flask and the cups.

'So . . . you're not at all worried by the earthquakes?' asked Tima. 'You don't think maybe you should put some . . . you know . . . props or something up in the caves and tunnels you've made . . . to stop them collapsing?'

'It's solid rock!' said Vardof, banging on the curved tunnel wall. 'It's not going to crumble.'

'You know that? You've studied the rocks around here?'

'Look, who are you? My mother? I know what I need to know,' he said, getting up and slinging his bag back on his shoulder. 'And the grubs know the rest.'

'Are you going to let us go?' demanded Jamie, trying to speak as clearly as he could.

Vardof got the gist this time. 'Sorry, boy,' he said. 'You're not going anywhere. Not until I've cleaned out this mountain range and shut my corridor.'

'How long will that take?' asked Tima, with a gulp.

He screwed up his face and counted across his fingers. 'Two or three weeks should do it,' he said. 'Then I'll let you both go. Probably. Not definitely. Maybe. If I still like you. I might kill you. See how it goes . . .'

CHAPTER 25

'How close are we?' asked Matt. 'Lucky's telling me we need to stop.'

'We'll stop soon—we're about twenty minutes away,' said Elena, consulting the map in the early light. It was nearly eight o'clock, a bright morning, and they'd been back on the road for ten minutes. They had managed to get some sleep and when they awoke their antlered guardian had left. 'We need to work out what we're going to say to Tima's mum and dad,' went on Elena, 'when we knock on the door . . . and probably find she's been at rehearsals in Edinburgh the whole time, perfectly fine.'

'We're not knocking on the door,' said Matt. 'We'll look for a window and send Lucky in. Or we'll see if we can connect with any spiders or beetles and find out what they know. We won't meet her parents unless we absolutely have to. Once we meet them they'll start asking questions . . . and they'll never stop.'

'Stop,' said Lucky.

'We could say we're on a school trip . . . and the coach was nearby and . . . no. There's no way they'll believe that,' sighed Elena. 'I keep trying to think of ways we could explain being here . . . maybe we hitch-hiked for fun . . . and got dropped off at a nearby truck stop.'

'Stop,' said Lucky.

'We won't meet them,' insisted Matt, going down a gear as they crested a high, sharp bend and began to descend into another idyllic valley, with a tumbling river and a loch gleaming at the bottom. 'We'll find Tima with our Night Speakers tricks or we won't find her at all. We can—'

'STOP!' shrieked Lucky, and Matt gave a cry of shock and slammed his foot on the brake as two massive raptors suddenly swooped right across the bonnet.

Elena screamed; she couldn't help it—the shock just whacked the shriek out of her as she rebounded in her seat, the belt snapping tight across her chest.

'Bloooo-dy hell! It's *you* again!' murmured Matt as a golden eagle thudded heavily onto the windscreen, grabbing the wipers with its talons; peering through the glass at him as its mighty wings flapped for balance. Its mate circled just above and let out a screech that made the hairs stand up on the back of Elena's neck.

'Back up!' she breathed. 'NOW!'

But Matt was already putting the Land Rover into reverse.

The eagle flapped up into the air as the vehicle juddered backwards at an alarming speed. Even through the rumble of the engine struggling uphill in reverse, Elena could *feel* it. The mountain road beneath them was *moving*. This wasn't just a distant rumble . . . the road was actually trembling and rolling, as if they were on some giant, loose rubber treadmill rather than a solid ribbon of tarmac. Elena grabbed hold of the strap above the window and clung on as the Land Rover bucked and wallowed. While Matt stared grimly over his shoulder at the road they were reversing along, Elena was fixated on the road in front, cold dread clawing at her throat.

As the crack appeared her mind went into a cartwheel of disbelief. The road was opening up! An ordinary British B road was *literally opening up in front of her*, like a cracked piecrust. 'MATT!' she bawled. 'MATT! LOOK!'

He brought the car to a juddering halt, wrenching on the handbrake, and turned his attention to the front windscreen and the unbelievable scene before them. The chasm across the road was at least a metre wide, juddering and writhing and sending up a cloud of dust. With a myriad of finer cracks radiating off it, it looked like a streak of lightning through the tarmac. Further down the mountain Elena saw a herd of deer running crazily from left to right. The loch in the pit of the valley was suddenly choppy with prickly, dancing waves. The shaking wasn't stopping.

'We need to turn around and drive back the way we came!' she breathed, still clinging to the strap.

Matt shook himself out of his freeze and threw the 4x4 back into gear, executing a fast three-point turn and heading back. He didn't get far. The eagles swooped low once more, each giving off an urgent screech and Matt slammed the brakes on again, causing Lucky to flutter frantically as she lost her footing on his headrest. 'I don't believe it,' he murmured.

Elena could barely believe it either. The shaking had ended ... but they were about four metres away from a *sheer drop*. The road hadn't just split open; it had dislocated entirely. A chasm as wide as their car lay before them; reddish grey dust rising up from it while small avalanches of stone, grit, and earth rippled down over the edges. The jagged tear through the mountain rose up to their left and tapered away between heavy boulders. They couldn't see how far down the valley to their right it went.

'Out!' said Matt. 'We've got to get out. Get all your stuff. We'll have to travel on foot.'

Shaking with fear and shock, Elena grabbed her warm coat, her backpack, and her gloves. 'Which way shall we go?' she asked, her voice high and scared. She could still feel occasional thuds and vibrations under her feet but the main quake seemed to be easing.

'Down the valley,' said Matt, shrugging into his coat and pulling his woollen hat over his hair. 'To the houses.' He pointed to a cluster of dwellings at the far end of the loch. 'That could be where Tima's place is.'

'I don't think so,' said Elena. 'It was another few miles on from here on the map ... but it *is* further along this valley, I think, so we might as well head for the houses; they're on our route.' She didn't add that she was longing, at this point, just to be near other people. Out here on the remote mountainside she was terrified that the earth would split asunder beneath their feet at any moment and swallow them . . . and nobody would ever know where they'd gone.

Matt grabbed her hand. He looked ashen but he pressed his lips flat together and drew in a long breath through his nostrils, steadying himself. 'Come on,' he said, slinging his bag over his shoulder. 'Stay close. Move fast. We can get there.' He glanced up at Lucky who was flying in loops around them, looking as disorientated as they felt. 'Stay up there!' he called to her. 'Follow us.'

There were a few more shakes as they stumbled down the slope, awkwardly supporting each other. Their booted feet tramped through springy heather one minute, then slid over loose gravel and rock and patches of snow the next. Behind them, the bus-wide chasm stretched down the valley for eight or ten metres, still sending up dust in puffs and spurts. Glancing over her shoulder, Elena could only guess at what was happening further down inside the mountain as that chunk of road surface tumbled and smashed and wrestled with loose rocks and fractured strata deep below. She half expected lava to shoot out in steaming orange fountains.

It can't, she told herself, *it's not a volcano! It's a Scottish mountain!*

Lucky coasted a metre or two above Matt's head. Much higher, the eagles turned a wide circuit and gave the occasional scream. It made Elena shiver. 'What are they telling you, Matt?' she said. 'I think I know but—'

'Keep moving,' grunted Matt. 'Just keep moving. It's not over.'

CHAPTER 26

'Vardof—please don't put us back in that little dark hole again,' begged Tima. 'Please! I want to find out more about your work. I mean . . . it's amazing. I've never seen anything like it. I want to know about the mining grubs; how they operate. We . . . we could *help* you, maybe. Help you get the job done quicker! We're strong and we learn fast.'

Vardof shot Jamie a sceptical look.

'He's a lot stronger than he looks!' said Tima. 'He's a farm boy. A Highlander.'

'Hmmm,' said Vardof, picking some meat-bread out of his teeth with a grimy fingernail. 'I don't need help. It'd be much easier to kill you.' He reached into one of his leathery pockets and pressed something and at once the grub's eye lit up and, with a steamy whistle, its jaws began to spin again.

'Please!' Tima screamed as the grub slowly trundled forward. 'Please don't kill us. You don't really want to . . . I mean . . . why give us food and water if you were going to kill us? You like us. You do!'

Vardof swung back around and glared at her from beneath shaggy dark brows. 'I don't like you,' he said. 'You're just a bit of entertainment. It's boring around here on my own. But that doesn't mean I won't kill you if you're too much bother. So shut up and get back in the hole.'

Tima stood in front of their might-be murderer and gave him the full benefit of her large brown eyes, brimming with tears. 'Vardof . . . we can't go back in that little hole. We *can't*. Please don't make us.'

He pressed inside his pocket again and the grub paused. He pursed his mouth, considering. 'All right,' he said. 'I'll bring another one in to seal the tunnel further down. You still can't go anywhere, but you'll have some space.' He gave a short, harsh laugh. 'You can use the hole as your toilet.'

Jamie gulped. He might need that toilet soon. His insides were quaking along with the ground beneath his feet. The tremors were coming along every other minute. This couldn't be normal . . . even deep inside a mountain.

'OK,' said Tima, with a faltering smile. 'Thank you. Thank you for giving us some space.'

Vardof turned his back on them and started stomping back down the tunnel. Tima went after him and Jamie followed. 'Vardof . . . how many grubs are there?' Tima called. 'Three or four?'

Vardof turned back, laughing. 'Four?'

Tima nodded.

'More like ninety four!' he chortled.

Tima glanced back at Jamie, her face full of shock and dread. When she turned back to Vardof her voice was low and controlled. 'Vardof . . . are you telling me that there are nearly a *hundred* grubs mining these mountains?'

He nodded. 'More or less. You've got to have a big number,' he said. 'They get through a lot of rock but I don't want any old grit—I want the precious stuff. I'm only taking about ten per cent of what they drop out the other end. Ninety per cent of it will get left on that moon.'

'How . . . how far have the grubs spread?' asked Tima.

'Oh, we've come quite a way,' said Vardof. 'It's quite a journey back to the corridor cave.'

Jamie gulped. He pictured the whole of Brawder's Pass— the familiar mountains and valleys he'd always known as his home—honeycombed with thousands of tunnels. No wonder the mountains were quaking. No wonder.

'But, what about—?' began Tima, but Vardof turned away again and stomped off, giving them a sharp backwards wave; he'd tired of the questions.

They followed in silence for a few more metres and reached the turn in the corridor that led into the huge cave they'd come through earlier. A steamy whistle went off and Jamie had a few seconds to see the grub in its full length as it turned a tight circle and came to seal their exit. It was five or six metres long, its shining silvery-pink skin in ringed segments, which contracted and expanded as the creature travelled. It had many tiny feet, too, like a millipede. It would have been just like a millipede, in fact, apart from the perfectly circular metal hoops attached to every segment, giving its soft, smooth body a steely exoskeleton. The whirring jaws were also like no millipede he'd ever seen. It was hard to tell whether these were the organic or the robotic part of the creature. The teeth looked like metal, but they weren't all precisely the same . . . as if they might have grown rather than been manufactured.

Jamie glanced at Tima as the grub turned its terrifying face towards them, steam shooting out from beneath it along with that weird whistle. They were both thinking about running, dashing out on one side or another before they were sealed in again.

But even if Tima could make it, he knew *he* couldn't. His left side was scrunched up like badly-worked plasticine. He was walking like a broken puppet. And Tima would never leave him behind to save herself. He *almost* wished she would . . . but being in this tunnel alone was unthinkable.

The grub sealed them in and then, thank god, its bright eye dimmed and its jaws stopped whirring. Tima sank down against the curved rock wall, close to the cyborg worm, resting her elbows on her knees and her head in her hands.

'It might be dangerous, being so near to it,' Jamie said. 'What if it starts up? What if it just decides to move?'

'It won't move unless Vardof tells it to,' sighed Tima. 'And if he does . . . if he decides we're too much trouble to keep here; to feed . . . well, we'll be done for. Even if we go back inside the hole . . . it can burrow right in after us if Vardof wants it to.'

The ground shook again and Jamie slid down the wall and sank onto the floor next to her. 'Sorry for getting you into this,' he muttered.

'No,' said Tima. '*I'm* sorry. It was my stupid idea to go running around in the night until we found stuff out. You would never have been so stupid on your own.'

The ground shook a little more.

'I'm going to use the toilet,' said Jamie.

CHAPTER 27

The ground stopped shuddering as they got closer to the village. Matt let go of Elena's hand. It seemed less likely they would be suddenly knocked off their feet. The loch, too, was calmer; the weird choppy waves had softened. He could see some people were outside, standing around in clusters and peering up at the mountainside.

Maybe it was all over. Maybe they could breathe out. He realized that the knots of people were looking up in his direction and one or two were pointing.

'They can see the birds,' said Elena. 'They're probably wondering why on earth a couple of golden eagles are chaperoning us down the valley.'

Matt glanced up and felt a thin smile on his face, breaking through the rigid mask of fear he'd been wearing for the past fifteen minutes. The golden eagles were a stunning sight; among the biggest raptors living free in the UK. Even up here in the Highlands a golden eagle sighting was rare and special; something tourists hoped for. As he thought this, he noticed the lodges and cottages looked quite touristy. There was a sign along one of the fences that bordered the narrow lane zigzagging down the mountainside. It read: **Glen Cawb Highland Holidays—lodges and cottages for rent**.

The eagles should probably leave them now, Matt thought. It was going to be tricky enough dealing with Lucky on his shoulder, without having to explain why two massive raptors were trailing them. He looked up and sent them the message: *It's OK—thank you! We're OK now.*

But the eagles continued to circle. Matt shook his head. There was nothing he could do about it.

'Whoa, up there!' called someone from below. 'Are you all right? Are you hurt?'

'No,' called back Elena. 'We're OK ... but we had to come down. There are big cracks up on the road.'

They reached a small knot of worried-looking people, one or two holding onto their pet dogs. The one who'd called out—a plump lady with grey hair curling out past her fur-lined hood—introduced herself. 'I'm Agnes; this is my holiday park. Did you get shaken about? You poor wee things—you must be terrified!'

'Yeah,' puffed Elena, smiling weakly. 'We are. Our car nearly went down a crack. Have you had earthquakes here before?'

'Weesht! No! It's a once in a millennium event!' said Agnes. 'It'll be all over the news. The loch started *shivering*. I've never seen anything like it. Looks like it's all over for another thousand years now, though.' She glanced around and smiled reassuringly at her guests who were beginning to look less worried; half of them had their mobile phones out, trying to get a signal to send someone the video they'd probably just been shooting.

'Don't think you'll get a signal,' said Matt. 'One of the transmitters was down across the A84. Others have gone over too, apparently.' He turned to look at the loch. It was flat but several long straight waves were rolling across it at an angle. It didn't look right. It didn't *feel* right. Nothing felt right. Still . . . at least the shaking had stopped. Maybe all he was feeling was a kind of emotional aftershock. He probably just needed a—

'Cup of tea?' asked Agnes. 'Come on into my lodge. You both look worn out. Where are your mum and dad? Did they stay with the car?'

'No,' said Matt. 'We're on our own. *I* drove. I'm seventeen. I know I don't look it, but . . .'

'Ach, no matter,' said Agnes. 'Come along in.'

Elena and Matt exchanged looks. Should they stop and have some tea? After the trauma of the quake it was a very appealing thought. Then a shaggy brown and white dog wandered across from its owner and wound around Elena's legs. Elena immediately dropped down to stroke the dog and communicate with it.

'You can bring your pet bird in too,' Agnes was saying. 'I don't mind.'

'Don't,' said Lucky. 'Mind.'

'Ach, listen to the wee birdy!' laughed Agnes. 'What is

that—a starling?'

'Yes,' said Matt, stroking Lucky's head as she rode on his shoulder. 'They mimic just like parrots do.'

'Don't,' said Lucky, as if she was arguing with him. Her small frame was thrumming with agitation.

Lucky, are we safe here? he sent to her.

'Matt,' said Elena, before he could catch Lucky's reply. She stood up and looked at him, her face set in a mask of worry. 'This boy isn't happy. He's not happy at all.'

'I've got some shortbread just about to come out of the oven,' said Agnes, going up the steps to her lodge and waving vigorously at them to follow.

'Come on,' said Matt. 'Let's talk inside.' He walked towards the lodge.

The dog barked shrilly. Matt glanced back. The dog's tail was well down and his ears flattened to his head. 'What's up, boy?' asked his owner, a middle-aged man wearing a deerstalker hat. 'You got spooked by the tremblies, eh?' He came to take the dog's collar and move him away to the neighbouring lodge but the dog crouched down and refused to walk.

'Don't,' said Lucky. Above her there were two piercing screeches.

'Well, look at *that!*' said the dog owner, looking up and spotting the eagles circling just a couple of metres above the roof of Agnes's lodge.

'MATT!' yelled Elena, her eyes wide and scared.

Matt spun around and yelled towards the lodge: 'AGNES! DON'T GO IN! COME OUT!'

There was no warning rumble or vibration this time; just a sudden thunderous crash, as if a herd of bison had stampeded through the tiny village. Elena screamed and grabbed his arm as the windows at the front of the lodge cracked and splintered, the frames twisted, the roof flipped up and back, scattering slate tiles left and right, and the whole building crumpled down into the earth, taking the neighbouring lodge with it.

They never even heard Agnes scream.

CHAPTER 28

'You need to relax,' said Tima.

'Relax?' repeated Jamie. 'Seriously?!'

'Yes. You're all twisted up,' she said. She'd been getting more and more worried about him. He wasn't saying much as the time wore on. His eyes were closed as he leaned against the tunnel wall in a spot equidistant from both of the grubs. In the standby light from each of their terrifying faces, he looked pale, and the left side of his mouth occasionally puckered, as if someone was tugging at it with invisible thread.

'Relax,' said Jamie, tilting his head to one side. 'We're deep inside a mountain, guarded by two ruthless killing machines which could mince us up at any moment, kept alive just as long as an alien pirate thinks we're entertaining ... in the epicentre of a non-stop earthquake. Why *wouldn't* I be relaxed?'

'Well,' said Tima. 'When you put it like *that* . . .'

He gave a mirthless chuckle.

'Come on—don't get down,' she said. 'We've still got my spider.'

'Oh yes. The spider.' Jamie rubbed his face with his good hand.

'She will have got a message out,' said Tima.

'To all the other spiders,' said Jamie. 'So . . . are they all going to build a massive web to catch the mining grubs? Is that the plan?'

Tima sighed. 'Well, sarcasm is better than moody silence, I suppose.'

'I'm not being sarcastic,' said Jamie. 'Well . . . OK, yes I am . . . but, you know, we *are* in a bit of a fix right now.'

'Well, I've been in worse fixes,' said Tima.

'Really?'

'Yes. At least the fate of the planet isn't resting on what I do next. And yes, the spider *will* get a message out.' She looked at the time on her mobile—8.43 a.m. 'I bet help is already on the way.'

'Any chance you've got a signal on that thing?' asked Jamie, flipping his own phone open and shaking his head at the No Service message.

'No,' said Tima. She had wandered around, holding her phone up high, but she knew there was little point. Who could get any cell coverage with tens, maybe hundreds of metres of solid rock all around them? At one point in the last couple of hours she had even dared to stand right up close to the dormant grub, holding the phone a centimetre from it, in case the metal or the electrical energy could give the signal a boost. It hadn't.

She was trying not to think about Mum and Dad. She knew they would be going crazy with worry. They must have discovered she was gone by now. They must be wondering what on earth had happened. Had they made any connection with the boy she had been hanging out with at the loch yesterday? Had they been in touch with Jamie's uncle and discovered Jamie was missing too? Was Hamish leading them to the hole in the mountain, even now?

The ground shook again and Jamie closed his eyes and bit his lips together, visibly holding on to his panic. Tima felt another twinge of guilt. Jamie would be safe at home or maybe at school if she'd just been a bit more thoughtful and a bit less *LET'S GO*. Her Night Speaker powers had made her stupidly overconfident; she saw this now. True, she and Matt and Elena had overcome some terrifying foes together, but Night Speakers weren't *actually* superheroes. They just happened to be able to communicate on a whole new level, since that random inter-dimensional beam first ran through their heads about seven months ago. She needed to stay chirpy and upbeat about the spider . . . but in truth her hopes were fading.

Then she felt something tickle her face and realized a friend had arrived. The moth was barely bigger than her thumb, which it now perched on. Its tiny feet clung to her skin as it slowly exercised wings of pale brown with dark brown bands.

'What's it saying to you?' asked Jamie, mov   cross t ake a look at the delicate insect.

Tima held the creature close to her face, focusing carefully. 'He says . . . *wow!*' She blinked and shook her head in wonder. 'He says my friends are close by. Elena and Matt . . . they're not far from here.' She blinked at him, astonished. 'They've come all the way from England!' She gulped. 'But they're in trouble.'

'What kind of trouble?'

As if in answer another deep tremor rumbled all around them and some grit showered from a crack in the smooth ceiling of the tunnel, a couple of metres away.

'*That* kind of trouble,' said Tima. 'We can't just sit around here waiting. It's telling me that too. We need to get out of here.'

'Great advice! Is it giving you any helpful tips on *how?*'

Tima closed her eyes and focused harder. 'Maybe,' she murmured. The insect was sharing a kind of mothnav with her. She could see it in vivid greens and blacks . . . a grainy map of their rock prison in three dimensions. She realized she was sensing the way this creature navigated in the full dark, when there was no moon to guide it—using magnetic fields. It was showing her all the available flying space in the tunnel, outlining the shape of the rock and even the conical faces of the grubs, motionless at either end of their prison. There was no obvious way out, but on one end—the end that led back to the main cave chamber—a little extra spur of space hung above the head of the grub. A natural air pocket inside the mountain meant not every bit of this tunnel was a perfect tube. She walked along a few steps, eyes up, and saw the shadow of the recess. It was just abo␢ the d␢␢␢l eyelight of the stationary grub. In theory, she ␢␢␢b's face and onto its back and move some way along it to reach that space; there *was* headroom.

In *theory*. But it would be madness to try. And even if she did, the tiny space wasn't a passage out of here. She would just be crawling along the grub and into a dead end. Except . . . *no* . . . the space was more than an arch over the grub's back . . . it was . . . a *shelf.* It led up into a space above a jut of rock. Water flowing through the natural caves had carved out passages over millions of years and left narrow slanting chimneys. This particular chimney connected to higher chambers and eventually up through a narrow sleeve in the mountain to the outside world. The moth had flown down to them through it. Unfortunately, you would need to be moth-sized to use it as an escape route but even so . . . it could be useful.

'Will we *both* fit in it?' she murmured.

If you make yourselves small, the moth told her.

And then what? What would they have achieved? Well, she told herself, if the grubs did suddenly power up and start to move in, she and Jamie would be out of harm's way. She turned to him, holding the moth aloft as it flexed its wings and prepared to fly away. 'How brave are you feeling?' she asked.

'How brave do I *look*?' he answered. 'You don't want to see what I left in that alcove.'

She grinned and nodded, as her little friend took flight.

'Why?' pressed Jamie. 'What are you thinking?'

The moth flitted up and vanished in the shadow just above the grub's head. Tima walked closer to the creature and narrowed her eyes, measuring it up. The circles of metal teeth were perfectly still and there wasn't even a hum running through it. But for the dim standby light still shining out from the centre of its face, it could have been made of stone.

The teeth whirls protruded at the centre in a kind of cone just below the eyelight . . . a bit like the pointed end of a screw, she reasoned. It would drive into the rock with that conical point and the rest of the teeth would follow. That shape meant it would be possible to climb the face of the grub; possible to clamber up it to the top where that shadow loomed. But what if the grub objected? What if it decided to spring into action and grind them into meat paste? Would it do that of its own accord? Even if it hadn't been told to by Vardof? Did it ever make its own decisions?

'Jamie,' she said. 'Do you think you could climb this?'

Jamie stood behind her and gazed up at the grub. He did not look keen. 'Why would I want to?' he asked.

'Because there's a hole above the tunnel . . . just up there. It's a safe place.'

Jamie looked unconvinced. 'It doesn't look safe.'

'Well, maybe it doesn't, but that moth flew all the way down from outside through that hole, just so it could tell us to get up there.'

'Can we escape through it?' Jamie's eyes lit up.

'No,' said Tima. 'It's too narrow further up. But we'd be safer up there than down here. If the grubs do start moving.'

'OK,' said Jamie. 'But how do we know this one won't start up as soon as we climb up. *I'd* kick off big time if someone climbed on *my* face.'

'We don't know,' sighed Tima. 'But do you really want to

sit here and wait to see whether we're going to be made into mincemeat? Or crushed by falling rock when the earthquake gets a bit closer?' As if in answer another prolonged tremor shook the tunnel and another cascade of grit showered down behind them.

Jamie shook his head. 'OK,' he said, with a gulp. 'I'll climb it. Stand back. Be ready to run if I get minced. Get back in the alcove. And, look, I'm sorry for the smell.'

Tima gave him a hug. 'No,' she said. 'That's not the plan. I am going to try to talk to it while you climb up. I will be right here.' She put her palm up on the eyelight, breathing slowly and working hard to give off calm vibrations.

'That's *so* not a good idea,' mumbled Jamie.

'It's the only idea we've got,' said Tima. 'So, shhhh, give me a few seconds and when I lift my left hand—climb!'

As she closed her eyes and leant sideways across the cone of teeth, resting her forehead against the domed light just above it, Tima realized she had never gambled so much on her faith in Night Speaking. This was an *alien creature;* a simple life form which was half animal, half machine. She had no idea whether it could *really* understand her; only the slightest instinct that it *might* . . . and that could be wishful thinking. She was playing Russian roulette with the ugliest of outcomes if she spun this wrong.

Are you in there? she sent.

Nothing.

Are you there? Can you sense me? Can you hear me?

Nothing.

Tima suddenly thought of the beam . . . the glorious golden stream of light and music which had messed up her life and changed her world. This creature had travelled into their world through a cave where that beam passed in and out daily. Had this grub felt the beam's presence? Did it rejoice in the music and the light the way she and Matt and Elena did?

Have you felt the beam? she asked it.

And it was *not* nothing. She felt the smallest flicker inside the creature's mind. A flicker of *recognition*.

It's so beautiful, isn't it? she asked.

Nothing for a several seconds and then . . . *Yes.*

Tima felt goosebumps wash across every part of her skin. She had *reached* it. She had reached the mining grub!

Do you want to experience the beam again? I do. I love it.

A pause . . . but not as long.

Yes.

Will you let us climb up over you?

The faintest hum of response.

Is that OK? Can we climb up and away? Out of danger?

Another hum, fizzing through the light into her forehead. *Yes.*

She raised her left hand. *Thank you,* she said, as Jamie began to climb.

CHAPTER 29

Elena's world was falling apart. Literally. She couldn't stop herself screaming as the ground gave way just a few steps from where she was standing. A huge crater had opened up and swallowed two wooden lodges in just a few seconds.

Above them the eagles whirled and screamed with her. The people who'd just begun to relax were back to shrieking panic too. The ground was shaking and rolling and sending up clouds of dust; nobody knew which way to run. The loch was once again a mass of glinting grey prickles as the water threw itself up and down in agitation.

'AGNES!'

Elena turned to see Matt clinging to a stout fence post and leaning over the newly born cliff edge.

'Lucky!' he yelled. 'Can you see her? Can you fly down and

see where she is?'

Lucky immediately dropped over the ragged edge of stone. The two eagles soared down after her; an impressive rearguard for a starling. Elena dropped to her hands and knees and crawled across to Matt, riding out the jolts and shudders as if she were a toddler on a bouncy castle. The roof of the lodge was visible, tipped over at a forty-five degree angle, two or three metres below the ground. Wooden beams, panels, and planks were sticking out in all directions and the only windows she could see were shattered and dark; one with a bright tartan curtain tangled in it.

Fearfully, Elena glanced around and saw the neighbouring lodge was in a similar position, crushed like a matchstick model in the lower reaches of the broken hillside to her left. Behind her, further down, two others had partially collapsed and slid several metres towards the anguished loch. Above her a telegraph pole was dancing back and forth, its wires pinging and snapping. As soon as she saw it she threw herself backwards, opening her mouth to bawl a warning to Matt.

She was too late. The heavy wooden pole was toppling. All she could manage was an incoherent shriek as it cracked down on top of Matt's head.

Only it never *hit* Matt's head.

Out of nowhere, the stag leapt in front of Matt, and butted the wood away with a glancing blow from its antlers. She sucked in her breath, terrified the creature would be poleaxed but it just knocked the post into the crater and shrugged one of the wires off its head.

Matt gaped up at it. 'Thanks,' he muttered. *'Thanks!'*

Elena crawled towards him again and then, carefully, stood up to put her arms around the thick red furry neck of the stag; the same that had kept them safe a few hours earlier. *'Thank you,'* she breathed. Beneath her feet the ground still spasmed and shook, but standing with her face buried in the stag's hide, she felt a huge pulse of strength.

'He's made a way for us to get down there,' she said to Matt.

The felled telegraph pole was now anchored in a V-shaped crag of exposed bedrock. Its upper end had flipped over and landed in the rubble of the lodge, forming a slanting bridge down past the chaos of rock and glass and splintered wood.

'You're not going down there!' grunted Matt. 'It's not safe.'

'It's not safe *anywhere!'* argued Elena. 'And nobody made *you* boss. We have to get Agnes out of there . . . if . . . if she's still . . .'

'She's alive,' said Matt, as Lucky shot up out of the ruins, the two eagles flapping energetically up behind her; they really were not suited to this kind of flying. 'AGNES!' he bawled. 'AAAAGNES!'

For a few seconds they heard nothing beyond the rumbling and the percussive cascade of dislodged pebbles and grit. Then, finally, the rocking stopped and they made out a faint cry.

'Are you OK?' yelled Elena. 'Are you hurt?'

'I . . . I've had better days . . .' came back the dry response. 'I think my leg might be broken.'

'Where are you?' yelled Matt.

'I don't know,' came the voice, wavering a little. 'It used to be the kitchen . . . but now I think it's the hallway as well.'

'Hang on! We're coming!' Matt turned to Elena. 'Handy impulse buy,' he said, pulling the tow rope out of his backpack. 'I'll go down,' he added, now getting out a headlight on a stretchy band and pulling it over his hat and down onto his brow.

'Wait,' said Elena. 'Matt – that's so dangerous.'

'Don't argue! There's not time. I need you up *here* with him,' he nodded at the stag. 'You'll both have to hold the rope and keep it steady if we get any more rock 'n' roll.'

Elena sighed and agreed. She consulted briefly with the stag and then looped the rope around its flank and under its forelegs, tying off across its strong, broad chest. Then she took the slack of the rope further along and held it firm in her fists and tight around both elbows, ready to share the load as Matt, with the other end tied around his waist, clambered over the edge of the crater and down onto the telegraph pole.

The pole was helpfully wedged and did not rock. There were metal struts along it, about a metre apart, presumably to help phone engineers climb it for repair and maintenance. Matt used these to climb down into the wreckage of the lodge. The doorway was crushed into a rhomboid shape, but there was still some kind of passage beyond it, tipping back in a steep slant. Matt reached the bottom of the pole, edging one stout boot out across the debris, which snapped and pinged and scraped but did not collapse any further.

He called again to Agnes and her reply came back, steady and strong, although she must be terrified. Matt carefully stepped across to the crushed doorframe and slid through it and out of sight. Elena picked up the slack of the rope, gulping with fear. It was terrible not to be able to see what was happening. How would she know if Matt stumbled through the broken walls or floor and into an even deeper hole?

Matt's muffled voice came up a few seconds later. 'We've got a problem!'

Elena glanced around, wondering if anyone else would come to help, but it seemed the others were busy panicking or taking action elsewhere. So . . . it was just her . . . and her stag. 'What do you need us to do?' she yelled back.

'Agnes is trapped under a bit of wood . . . a big bit. Part of the roof timber,' came back Matt's voice. 'I can't lift it. I'm going to tie my rope to it and then you and the stag . . . you'll have to pull, OK?'

'But . . . what about you? Without that rope attached you—'

'This is NOT a discussion!' yelled Matt. 'I'm doing it now.'

Elena felt the rope tug and swing and vibrate along its length. She took a steadying breath. Matt was only doing exactly what *she* would do if she were down there now. She had to trust him.

'OK! PULL NOW!'

She and the stag moved back until the rope was taut. They kept going until it was thrumming with stress, pulling against something very, very heavy. Or perhaps trapped by a boulder—who knew?

'We can't go any further!' she shrieked back. 'It's stuck.'

'No—it's good—you're holding it up. Keep it still!' bawled back Matt, the strain obvious in his voice 'I'm trying to move

Agnes out from under the wood . . . Just . . . stay . . . there.'

Elena and the stag pulled back, anchored their feet in the gritty, troubled earth. She prayed there would be no more quaking. If there was she might lose her grip and a whole wall or ceiling might topple in and crush Agnes or, worse, Matt. The stag was straining too—and nervous. It wanted to be with its herd. It had taken immense courage for it to leave its own kind and come to her aid again—and she hadn't even *asked*. The tight twist of rope was burning into her palms and knuckles, turning her fingers blue. She wondered if the stag could take up the slack in time if she eased one off it, but she just didn't dare. It could be catastrophic. She only hoped she would regain full use of her hands once this nightmarish struggle ended. *If* it ended.

Then she heard another shout and could see a grey head bob up through the crushed door frame.

'KEEP HOLDING!' called Matt. 'If you let go the whole thing's going to crash down. And there's a big drop under it. Just hang on a bit longer until we're clear!'

Elena gritted her teeth and felt tears of pain flow down her cheeks. She really shouldn't have looped that rope around her hand. Behind her the stag, sensing her pain, softly nuzzled the back of her head in sympathy, making her cry even more. She noticed, suddenly, that there was more help. The dog and its owner had emerged from the chaos and were at the edge of the crater. The man reached down and helped Agnes to clamber slowly up the pole, calling out words of comfort while the dog barked encouragement.

'Are you OUT?' Elena called to Matt, her voice a rasp of pain.

'NEARLY!' he called back. 'Hang on just a few seconds more. You can do it!'

Agnes stumbled over the lip of the crater and into the arms of the dog owner. Then, thank *god*, Matt's head emerged and he scrambled up and collapsed onto the ground, gasping and clutching his right hand to his left shoulder. 'Let it go now,' he croaked.

Elena and the stag eased forward; the rope slackened. She quickly undid it from the animal's neck and chest. Then, just as she was daring to breathe out, there was another almighty crash and the rope, still looped around her wrist, suddenly yanked her forward and flat on her face. It dragged her relentlessly towards the edge as she desperately tried to detach herself. Matt gave a shout of alarm but there was no time for him to help. She was going to go over.

A thud of hoofs sounded by her head and then a heavier thud as the stag dropped in front of her and halted her slide with its body weight. Shielded and pinned down safely, she wriggled out of the loop of rope at last. 'It's OK,' she gasped. 'Let it go!' And the stag shifted its ribcage, allowing the rope to slide out under it and vanish into the crater amid more crashes and rumbles and cascades of grit and rock.

It got nimbly to its feet and backed away from the edge, tossing its head, eyes wild with fear. Elena ran to it and patted her wounded hand against its neck. 'Thank you. You were *so* brave,' she murmured, sniffing back tears. 'You must go back to your herd now. They need you.'

But the stag stayed where it was.

'Is Agnes OK?' Elena asked.

Matt was sitting up now, looking as wrecked as she felt, his hand still clamped to his shoulder. There was blood oozing between his fingers.

'What happened?' she said, going to him.

He shook his head. 'It's nothing much. I just got snagged on one of the nails in a bit of broken timber. It's fine.'

'It's not fine,' said Elena. 'I'll get some bandage on it.'

'Not yet. We've got to get somewhere safer first,' said Matt.

'Where the hell is safer?!' Elena squeaked.

'Are you all right, lad?' Agnes asked. She was standing now, supported by the dog owner, testing her leg. Her hair was full of dust and grit and there was a bruise on her cheek and big rips in her coat, but she looked remarkably together.

'I'm fine,' said Matt. 'How about you?'

'Ach, I'll live,' she said. 'My leg's not too grand but I don't think it *is* broken. Just bruised . . . sprained ankle, maybe. Has anybody dialled 999 yet? Are we getting helicopters and the like?'

'Aye,' said the dog owner. 'My son has a satellite phone. Help is on the way.'

'Is anyone else trapped?' asked Elena, gently moving her bruised fingers, which were aching even more intensely as the blood began to flow back into them.

'No, we're all accounted for,' said the man. 'We were all outside when the quake struck. Listen to me! A *quake!* Here in Scotland. I cannae believe it! What's going on? It's nae natural around these parts!'

Matt looked at Elena. 'It isn't natural,' he said, quietly, as Lucky settled on his woollen cap, careful to avoid his painful shoulder.

She leaned in closer, taking off her backpack and getting some bandage from its small first aid pouch. 'What did you see down there?'

'The floor had fallen through on one side . . . we were hanging over some kind of . . . tunnel. It's round . . . like a tube station. I shone my torch down there. It's *perfect*—like it's been cut with a massive drill. Something industrial . . . There's nothing natural about it.'

'A massive drill . . . turning in a circle?' said Elena, easing his torn sleeve off and wrapping some lint and a bandage around the deep puncture wound. 'Spinning?'

'Yes. That.' Matt closed his eyes, exhausted.

'What do we do now?' asked Elena, sticking the bandage down firmly with tape and sitting back on her heels.

Matt glanced up behind her at the stag.

'I think you'd better ask *him*.'

Elena looked up to see the eagles still coasting in lazy arcs above them. 'And *them*. They're going to direct us on, aren't they? To find Tima.'

CHAPTER 30

The circular jaws of the grub did not move as Jamie climbed up its face. Tima could see he was shaking with terror and she didn't blame him. It was like climbing into a food mixer with a dodgy on/off switch. They could be pulped at any moment. But, despite his left side clenching and juddering in panic, Jamie managed to get up onto the grub's head in just a few seconds.

'Are you OK?' she called up after him.

'Oh yeah,' he called back. 'Nothing quite like fear of instant death to get you moving. Remind me to tell my physio about this!'

Tima hauled herself up next and found Jamie clinging to the smooth dome of metal which capped the grub's head. She clambered closer to him, careful to avoid braining herself on the rock just above. Beyond the grub's head she could see the segments of its organic part . . . the skin. She hadn't got her torch out yet but she didn't need to . . . the grub had its own gentle pink glow, suffusing through its body, revealing a network of tiny purple thread-like veins.

'It's breathing,' whispered Jamie, pointing to the gentle swell and contraction of the skin under the metal hoops.

Tima glanced up and saw the shelf of rock and the dark gap above it, just as the moth had described it in her head. All they had to do was reach across and pull themselves up into it. She nudged Jamie. 'Go on,' she said. 'You first.'

Jamie nodded and lurched forward, grabbing the rough lip of the shelf. He landed on his knees, and scrambled up the slope into the darkness. Tima waited until he'd cleared some space and then did the same, somewhat more nimbly. Jamie climbed on and then grunted with pain as his head struck where the slanted ceiling met the floor. That was it. No more space. Tima tucked her legs under her, only just out of sight of the tunnel below.

She scrunched up on the shelf and muttered: 'Are you—?' Then her words were drowned out by a sudden, steamy, whistling vibration. Tima stared down at it in shock. Was the grub backing up? Was Vardof coming in to check on them?

No. Tima shook her head, staggered and barely able to believe it as the spine of the grub moved along and out of sight in the opposite direction. 'It's moving *in!*' she gasped. 'It's goi up to the other one. He killed us! He actually *killed* us!'

Jamie didn't reply. Tima scrabbled for her torch and th their tiny cavern. Jamie was hunched up awkwardly at th of it, his head low under a craggy outcrop. He looked s knew why. If he had taken one more minute to be convinced to climb up the grub, they would now be dead. Horribly dead.

'I didn't think he would. I didn't think he would do it!' murmured Tima, shaking her head. 'How *could* he?'

'Sssssh!' Jamie grabbed her shoulder. 'Listen!'

As the rumbling grew quieter, voices floated in. Not below them but somewhere above. The slanting chimney they were crouched in might not offer them an escape but there was a passage, wide enough and long enough to channel back voices.

'. . . do that for? You didn't need to do that!'

The voice was familiar and sounded put out. It was Vardof. But who was he talking to? Himself? With those sudden wild bursts of laughter he'd kept breaking into earlier, Tima could well believe the alien pirate wasn't entirely sane. Then another voice answered; low and measured. 'It's for the best. You're too soft.'

'They were only kids,' grunted Vardof.

'If you'd let them go they'd just have gone whining to their parents,' replied the new arrival. 'We don't need that. It's time to pack up and get out of here.'

'But, Raxus, I've hardly even got *started!*' whined Vardof. 'There's a *fortune* in minerals in these mountains. A *fortune!* Jasper, marble, sapphire, amethyst, even gold and ruby! I've only just mined the jasper.'

There was another juddering quake at that point, and Jamie ed Tima's arm, and furrowed his brow at her. *'What are they* 'he hissed.

're arguing about killing us,' she whispered back,

suddenly aware that she was listening into a brand new language—from another galaxy. 'Vardof didn't want to . . . this new guy, Raxus, wanted us out of the way. Shhh now. I have to listen.'

'—earthquakes?!' Raxus was saying. 'This is not an earthquake zone.'

'Well, no . . .' said Vardof.

Raxus gave a low growl. 'You idiot. You haven't used any prop fungus, have you?'

'Prop fungus? *What* is prop fungus?'

Raxus muttered a series of oaths and then went on, as if he was addressing a particularly dim toddler. 'You have to use the prop fungus to support the great big HOLES you're making. Or else the mountains will FALL ON YOUR HEAD!'

'I didn't *know* about prop fungus,' whined Vardof. 'Nobody told me. I don't even know what it looks like. I didn't see any fungus lying around on the freighter.'

Raxus sighed heavily. 'It's in the storage bay marked PROP FUNGUS! It's in powder form. You load the grubs' tails with the powder canisters and they spray the tunnels as they dig them. Then the fungus grows . . . very fast because that's w prop fungus *does* . . . and the network props up any weak in the tunnels.'

'There aren't any weak points,' said Vardof, stou ridden all the way through these caves and it's a' rock.'

'So why . . .' There was a pause as another s struck. '. . . is this mountain shaking? And why collapsed tunnels on route 58 on my way through to you? And why is a drowned grub floating in one of the lower chambers on route 203?'

'A *drowned grub?*' echoed Vardof.

'Yes. You've lost one. It punched through into a body of water; one of the lochs. You've been getting a lot of punch-throughs, haven't you? How many grubs have breached since you've been running this mining mission? How many have been *seen?*'

Vardof coughed. 'Look . . . I never said I was an expert. I just said I could get by. It's worth the risk. We're going to be rich. We've just got to get all the grubs back to the key cave and through the corridor.'

'And here's the problem with *that*,' said Raxus. 'You didn't check the debris storm calendar.'

'Debris storm?' Vardof sounded rattled. 'What debris storm?'

'You see, little brother,' went on Raxus, 'you never look at the detail, do you? You just jump right in. There is a *reason* why that Cornelian moon is uninhabited. Haven't you ever wondered about that, when the atmosphere is perfectly breathable?'

'Why?' grunted Vardof, sounding sulky.

'It's on a storm belt,' said Raxus. 'Storms hit it regularly. [s]torms. And the next one is due to hit in the next 24 Earth [hours]. if we don't get back there, load up as much as we can, [. . . t]he surface, we won't have a ship to go back to. Just a [twiste]d metal.'

[. . . ex]haled Vardof. 'It'll take me half a day to get all [. . .] [A]t least!'

[. . . go]ing to happen,' said Raxus. 'We need all that

time just to load up the minerals already there. It's just the two of us, remember, not a whole crew! So we take what we've already got and leave the grubs down here behind.'

'But . . . just . . . *leave* them here?'

'Yes. Set them free. They've got plenty to live on. They can go on eating through this mountain range forever. They can have baby grubs and live in paradise—assuming they don't get flattened by the earthquakes they trigger.'

'But what about the prop fungus? There are people up there—'

'Not our problem now, brother. You're too sentimental. It's time to go.'

Vardof continued to protest but his voice grew fainter as the pair of them walked away. Tima glanced at Jamie, as he raised his palms at her questioningly. How could she tell him the mountains he grew up in were going to be riddled with tunnels until they collapsed . . . very likely swallowing his home?

'Not good news, then?' he said, taking in her expression. 'Whatever it is, it can wait. We need to get down into the tunnel before the grubs come back. They went upwards . . . so we're not blocked in now. We can escape!'

Tima felt a surge of adrenalin. 'Of course!' she said. 'Let's go.' She crawled to the edge of the rock ledge and shone her torch down into the tunnel which was much darker now the light from the grub had gone; just a dim glow seeped into it from the direction they needed to travel—the big chamber they'd last been in hours ago. Below her was a drop of about three metres.

'Slide your legs over and dangle down as far as you can before you drop,' she said. 'It's not that far to fall but it's solid rock under so make sure you bend your knees as you land!'

Jamie rolled his eyes at her. 'Just because I sound like an idiot, doesn't mean I *am* one,' he said. 'I have jumped off things before.'

'OK, OK . . . I was just checking you knew!' she muttered and then eased herself over the edge and dropped.

Jamie followed her surprisingly quickly. She noticed he wasn't quite as scrunched up down one side as before. They sprinted down the tunnel towards the large chamber and Jamie grabbed her arm and pulled her to a halt just as a rumbling, steaming grub trundled past them across the wide cavern floor. They flattened themselves against the tunnel wall until it had passed. Tima wasn't convinced it would react to them anyway; these simple beings seemed only to do as they were instructed.

'So . . . are you going to tell me the dreadful thing?' puffed Jamie, as the grub disappeared into another tunnel. Tima looked at her feet. 'Come on. I could tell from your face that what those two aliens were saying wasn't exactly happy news.' Jamie fixed her with his dark green eyes and tightened his jaw. He was not going to be put off. 'What is the dreadful thing you're not saying?'

'We have to do something,' said Tima. 'Because they're going. They're leaving this planet and they're not coming back.'

'Isn't that good news?' asked Jamie.

'Er—no. They're leaving the mining grubs behind,' she said. 'And . . . the grubs won't stop. Not ever. They'll just go on tunnelling and tunnelling . . . until the mountains fall.'

CHAPTER 31

A thudding through the air told Matt it was time to go. They'd lost half an hour in the village, rescuing Agnes and then getting way too much attention from everyone in the midst of this drama. Even with an emergency helicopter hanging over the valley, people were eyeing the stag and the eagles with wonder and fascination. Wild animals could behave oddly during natural disasters, but fixedly sticking around two teenage kids was very odd. Any normal wild animal would have fled to its own kind by now.

As the chopper moved towards the stricken village and its downdraft began to whip everyone's hair around their faces, Matt grabbed Elena's arm. She glanced at him and nodded. Now was the time. While everyone was focused on the emergency services they probably wouldn't notice the young strangers sneaking away along the valley with an apparently tame and helpful stag and the airborne tag team of a couple of golden eagles and a starling. The stag took the lead in seconds, guiding them along a path which rose and fell among the heather and rocky outcrops, while the pair of raptors circled high overhead, screeching occasionally, and Lucky fluttered close to Matt. Matt couldn't explain to anyone other than Elena and Tima *how* he knew it, but he did know that the eagles were scouting, telling the stag and Lucky and the two Night Speakers which areas to avoid.

It was a good thing, too. Within minutes of starting their journey they were guided abruptly onto a higher, more difficult ridge, where a hardened crust of snow clung to the vegetation. Glancing down the valley as they clambered over a slab of granite, Matt saw that the lower path had dropped into a newly torn ravine. Red dust was still rising from the gap, which was at least two metres across; it had clearly only just happened. He felt another tremble beneath his feet and pushed on up the slope at greater speed. The tremble faded and the ground they were climbing now felt solid enough, especially when they reached another stretch of narrow tarmac—the same road they'd been marooned on further back along the ridgeway. This one looked smooth and undamaged . . . he just hoped it wouldn't open up and eat them.

'This thing,' said Elena, catching her breath for a moment as they walked across the road and on up the slope after their four-legged guide. 'This thing the stag has seen . . . it's . . . like a machine, isn't it?'

Matt nodded. He'd been getting the glimpses too. Whatever the stag had seen, it was doing its best to convey the image whenever it paused and waited for them to catch up with it; little telepathic flashes were leaping from the animal's mind to theirs, along with its sense of shock and panic. Matt could make out the herd, leaping away in terror and one deer shuddering in its death throes on the mountainside; a perfect round hole driven through it, chopping it in two. He could see the hole in the rock just behind the dying deer, and catch a blink of something spinning and steaming inside. He wasn't at all sure he *wanted* to ever meet that thing; dealing out its perfectly circular death.

So thick was his sense of dread that he almost screamed aloud when something rotating and chopping rose up above the peak that hung over them. It had come out of nowhere, gleaming white with a flashing red light. On its side were the letters ITN.

'It's a media chopper!' yelled Elena, covering her face as her hair whirled around her head.

Matt ducked away under a springy overhang of vegetation, cursing and pulling Lucky from her perch on his hat and holding her close against his chest. Elena scooted in after them as the stag fled. Glancing up through dead brown prickles of thistle Matt could see the cameraman actually filming them at this very moment. The hovering machine was so close to the mountain it was flattening the wiry grass and heather.

'Go away! Go AWAY!' Elena was yelling. 'Matt!' She turned to look at him as they crouched together. 'We CAN'T let them film us! We can't be all over the news! What if your dad sees it?'

'ARE YOU TWO OK?' The chopper had a loudhailer with

enough volume to slice through the noise of its rotors.

Matt stuck out a hand, making a thumbs up gesture.

'IT'S NOT SAFE UP HERE!' went on the loudhailer voice; female by the sound of it. 'YOU NEED TO GET AWAY HOME TO SAFETY!'

Matt made a circle with his thumb and forefinger, hoping they would read the gesture and take it to mean he and Elena were OK and heading home—and just fly away. The chopper continued to hang in the air and the lens of the camera glinted in a shaft of late morning sun. Was it zooming in on their faces? Had it already caught them before they'd got under cover? Matt was wondering whether to ask the eagles, still circling above, to distract it when there was another rumble and further down the valley some more dust rose up. 'DID YOU GET THAT?' said the woman on the loudhailer and the chopper spun instantly in the air and then darted away down the valley to film something more exciting.

The stag seemed to have gone, scared away by the helicopter—but they didn't have much further to go or any other direction to take. Elena stumbled ahead, looking exhausted and Matt knew he couldn't be looking much better. He thought wistfully of that cup of tea and shortbread that poor Agnes had offered them moments before her home collapsed into a crevasse. Up here, in the middle of a remote and shaking mountain range, it was hard to believe he would ever sit down and drink a cup of tea again.

But finally, they arrived in an area a few metres below the peak; a small basin in the rock and heather, sheltered from wind by a high rock wall on one side. Matt could imagine a herd of deer here, contentedly cropping the wiry turf between patches of snow.

Elena was walking along beside the rock face, pressing her hands to it at waist height. 'It was here,' she said. 'Right here.'

'I'm getting that too,' agreed Matt.

'I'm getting that too,' echoed Lucky, from his shoulder.

'But where is the way in?' Elena asked, still patting along and peering at the wall of mountainside. 'There's nothing here.'

Matt pressed along with his hands too. Elena was right. There was no hidden entrance here. He yelled out in frustrated rage and slumped down against the rock wall. Had they really come all this way for *this*? For *nothing*? They were meant to be rescuing Tima but they had no idea where she was. This whole exercise was for nothing. He had stolen a car and left it stranded on a wrecked mountain road. He'd dragged Elena along too and put her in incredible danger. At any moment another earthquake might split the ground beneath them. Even if they somehow managed to get out of all this, there was every chance he and Elena would be shown on the ITV news that very evening, in full colour close-up. And whether that happened or not, his dad would probably punch him into a coma when he got back home without the Land Rover.

Matt lifted his face and let out a volley of swear words, concluding in a howl of frustrated rage.

There was moment of silence as Elena stared at him.

'Yeah,' she said. 'That.'

CHAPTER 32

Jamie and Tima ran back up the tunnel they'd first come down, following the light of Tima's torch. At least, Jamie *hoped* it was the same tunnel. He also hoped they wouldn't meet a grub at the end of it, heading straight for them. There were exit points along it that he hadn't noticed earlier when they'd been travelling down it for the first time. There hadn't been any quaking for a while but he was sure he heard whistling and rumbling as they ran past two of these exits.

'Are we in the right tunnel?' he puffed, close on Tima's heels.

'Yes. I'm sure of it!' she puffed back. 'My glove—yeah?' She waved the glove she'd grabbed from behind the rock as they'd run past.

'But shouldn't we be able to see some light by now? Daylight ... from where we came in?'

Tima slowed down, looking less sure of herself. 'Maybe . . . I think . . .'

There was a whistle and they both froze. A beam of light suddenly shone out across the tunnel at an angle, a few steps back the way they'd come. A grub was coming. They stared at each other in horror and began to run wildly on. Behind them the steaming, whistling noise grew louder and the light brighter, but, glancing back over his shoulder, Jamie saw the grub emerge and then turn *away* from them, heading back down the tunnel towards the main chamber. He let out an immense sigh of relief at the sight of its curved, pale pink back end trundling away.

'Wait a moment,' said Tima. 'What's that on the back of it?'

Jamie peered along the torch beam Tima was casting across the retreating rear of the grub. There was something shining and metallic along the base of the creature. It was gently curving on its vertical plane and quite flat on the horizontal. A metre or so above it was a metal . . . rail . . . ? Was that a *handrail?*

'It's a footplate!' he murmured. 'Like . . . like the back of an old-fashioned steam train or bus.'

'That's what it looks like,' said Tima. 'It looks like you can . . . *ride* it.'

'But why would you want to?' said Jamie.

Tima shrugged. 'It doesn't matter. We have to get out of here. Go and get some help.'

They turned and headed back up the tunnel, scanning every side exit in the curved walls for the glow of a grub's eye and listening intently for the steaming, whistling warning.

'We should be seeing the light by now,' said Jamie. 'There's no way we walked this far down from the hole before. Where is it? We must be in the wrong tunnel.'

Tima dropped to her knees. 'No. This *is* the tunnel. We were definitely here.' She held up a scrap of paper; a sweet wrapper. 'This was in my pocket,' she said.

They reached the funnel end of the tunnel and found nothing but rock.

'This makes no sense!' wailed Jamie. 'If we came through here, how come it's solid rock?'

'Unless it's *not* solid,' Tima said. 'Remember the trapdoor spider. It just *looks* like solid rock.

Elena wanted to cry. But she didn't have the energy. 'What now?' she murmured. 'What do we do now?'

'So much for the call of the wild,' muttered Matt, his back to the wall of rock and his chin on his chest. Even the eagles had abandoned them.

'So . . . we know Tima is around here somewhere,' said Elena, trying not to lose it. She had never been so scared and so tired for so long. 'We just need to—'

The stag suddenly crested the top of the mountain and walked down to them.

'He's back!' beamed Elena. But the stag paid her no attention. It walked down towards Matt and stared at him.

'Am I . . . in your way?' he asked.

The stag gave a snort and pawed a hoof on the ground. Matt got up and moved aside.

Then the stag drove its antlers into the rock.

Matt and Elena gaped as the wall of granite shattered.

A few seconds later a dark head emerged from the hole in it and said: 'Well . . . *you* took your time.'

CHAPTER 33

'So . . . any of you any good at the long jump?' Matt stared down into the deep crevasse that had opened up halfway along their route back down. It was at least three metres wide and four or five times as deep.

'I wonder what happened to Hamish?' said Tima, gulping. 'He must have gone to get help hours ago . . . maybe this is why he hasn't come back.'

'It's OK, he's not down there,' said Elena, peering over the edge. Tima relaxed, knowing any number of small furry creatures in the area might be communicating this intel to her friend.

'We'll have to find another way down,' said Matt. 'But let's have some food first. Your mate looks like he's ready to drop,' he said to Tima.

'He's tougher than he looks,' she said.

They all settled into the shelter of an overhang of rock as Elena and Matt pulled their backpacks off and started handing round food and water.

'So . . . there are ninety-odd alien grubs slowly eating all the rock underneath us,' said Elena, halfway through a sandwich and shaking her head in disbelief. 'What are we going to do?'

'Do we *have* to do anything?' asked Matt, unexpectedly. He was keeping his head down and his woolly hat pulled low over his brow, in case another media helicopter flew their way; they could see a black speck hovering in the distance. 'I mean . . . it's not exactly a secret is it? The emergency services are already here!'

'But they don't know what's causing the quakes,' said Tima. 'They need to know about the grubs.'

'Tell us again . . . what they're like,' said Elena. 'Describe them.'

'They're about the size of a big minibus I'd say,' said Tima. 'They're partly animal—their skin is greyish pink—in segments, like a caterpillar. They've been put—or maybe *grown*—inside a sort of cage . . . rings of metal all the way along. Their faces are terrifying—all spinning teeth below a big white lamp which I think is their eye.'

'Sounds like a nightmare,' said Elena.

'Tell her about the footplate,' prompted Jamie, finishing a service station sandwich and rolling his eyes with pleasure; they'd eaten very little in the past few hours.

'You tell her,' said Tima.

'She won't understand me,' said Jamie, sighing. 'To everyone else but you, I just sound like I'm talking through a potato.'

Elena laughed. 'I'd say it's more like you're talking through a mouthful of bread and cheese.'

Jamie blinked in surprise. 'You mean . . . she's a Night Talker too?' he asked Tima.

'Night *Speaker*,' corrected Elena. 'Yes. We all are—Matt too.' Matt nodded, stroking Lucky who was roosting on his fist. 'We can all understand any language on the planet,' Elena went on. 'And a few *off* the planet too. Animal language is the best, though.' She smiled, glancing over at the stag. It had followed them down the mountainside and was now grazing nearby. 'Tima's thing is insects and spiders, Matt is brilliant with birds—and me . . . I'm all about the mammals. But we can speak to any animal at all; any of us.'

Jamie rubbed his face. 'My brain is flipping out.'

'Yeah,' said Matt. 'Join the club.'

'Anyway, what about the footplate? What do you mean?' asked Elena.

'Well—there's this metal bit on the back of the grubs—a kind of step—and a metal rail too,' said Jamie. 'It looks like whoever made them designed them so you could ride on the back.'

'That would be some ride,' said Matt. 'The cavers will have a blast when they find *that*.'

'Look—I don't know why you think we should just give up and hand it all over to the authorities,' snapped Tima. She was tired and she didn't have much tether left. 'All they'll do is go nuts and then try to kill all the grubs. And there are *ninety* or more of them burrowing around down there. How long before the whole mountain range collapses? And as soon as people start going down there, how many will get killed? If the grubs have run right through deer and cows, they can easily run right through people. Also—even if the authorities somehow catch them and stop them ... how are they going to fix all the unstable tunnels?'

'Do you think your space pirates might come back?' asked Elena. 'After they've got their spaceship away from the meteor storm? They might come back through the corridor. They might take the grubs away.'

'They *might*,' said Tima. 'But they might not. They didn't sound like the most organized people. And in the meantime, this whole mountain range is going to collapse—maybe the entire Highlands if those grubs eventually start breeding. The whole area could just end up a massive quake zone.'

As if to underline her doom-laden words, another rumble ran through the earth beneath them.

'So ... what are we meant to do?' asked Matt. 'Because I can't see how we can help. We're not superheroes. We can't fight these things. And ...' he ducked his head low as another helicopter looped around the valley a little too close, '... *we're* not even meant to *be* here.'

'He took a car from Kowski Kar Klean,' Elena explained.

Tima winced. Oh no. Things were *not* going to go well for Matt when he got home.

Matt screwed up his empty sandwich packet. 'Whatever plan you've got, Tee, we can't do much about it anyway. Not if we're stuck up here. There might *not* be another way down.'

'We could always wave at the helicopters,' suggested Jamie. 'Get rescued.'

'No!' said Matt and Elena, in unison.

'We're not meant to be here,' added Elena.

'Well . . . Matt's in trouble *wherever* he's spotted,' pointed out Tima.

'I know,' said Elena. 'But there'll be SO much explaining to do. We can't exactly tell the police that golden eagles and squirrels told us to get here on the double . . .'

'Yeah, OK,' agreed Tima.

'Well, you'd better come home with me then,' said Jamie. He got to his feet, grinning, and began to wave.

Tima stood up next to him and spotted the battered old Jeep driving up the road to the far side of the newly born crevasse. Out of it got a man and a dog. The man went to the back of the Jeep and pulled out . . . what was that? An extendable ladder!

'Hamish took his time,' said Jamie. 'But he didn't let us down. Come on.'

They began to climb down the mountainside, carefully working their way across loose rock and grit and patches of thin frozen snow. Jamie's uncle, dressed in warm winter clothing and a woollen hat, lay the ladder down and extended it across the crevasse. It reached the other edge with a couple of rungs to spare and he worked it from side to side until it found a stable resting place. Hamish, close to Fraser's side, whined anxiously and lowered himself to the ground, ears pricked and eyes darting around. Tima sent him a message as they got closer: 'We're OK.

We'll all be OK.' In response the collie glanced across at her and allowed his tail to thump once on the ground. He wasn't convinced. Nor, to be honest, was Tima.

'You'll need to hold it steady at your end,' Fraser yelled across. 'It should hold fine—but crawl across slowly, on your belly—spread your weight evenly.'

Matt pinned the end of the ladder down and waved for Tima to go, but she shook her head. 'No,' she said. 'You need to go first—then Elena—then Jamie. I'm small and light so that ladder won't shift around too much when I cross. You're heavier, Matt—we need to be pinning the ladder down at this end to stop it from tipping sideways.'

Matt opened his mouth to protest but the man at the other end called over: 'She's right. You and I can secure the ladder at just one end for her—but it'll need steadying both ends for you. You need to come now, lad!'

Matt shrugged, shook his head, and then got to his knees, reaching across the ladder. As soon as he'd clambered onto it, Elena, Tima, and Jamie pinned the metal rungs to the ground. Tima tried not to glance down into the crevasse. It was shadowy and she had no idea how long the drop was—did it end in a grub tunnel?

The ladder wobbled and dipped alarmingly as Matt worked his way across it. They all grunted and shoved one side of it down hard as it threatened to tilt and tip Matt into the darkness below. But Matt just kept moving, working his arms and legs and slithering to the other side. He clambered off and they heard his gruff: 'Thanks.' Then he turned around and helped their rescuer to steady the ladder for Elena.

'I don't like leaving you here,' muttered Elena. '*I* should go last.'

'Shut up and get on that ladder!' said Tima. 'Now!'

Elena grinned at her friend. 'All right, titch. Keep your hair on!' She took a deep breath and then followed Matt. She got across quickly, with much less ladder tilting, even though only Tima and Jamie were now pinning down their end.

Jamie started to go through the same performance when it was his turn. 'I think I should go last—'

'Give it a rest, Sandpaper Boy!' said Tima. 'You don't want to have one of your spasms halfway across with only one side of this ladder held down. Get moving!'

Jamie shook his head. 'It's discrimination,' he muttered, but he did as he was told. It took him longer to get over and the tension on his uncle's face was clearly visible to Tima, even at the other end of the extended ladder. At one point Jamie looked down between the rungs and froze for quite a few seconds, squeezing his eyes shut.

'You can do it,' said his uncle. Jamie opened his eyes. He looked straight ahead and began to move again. He reached the far side half a minute later.

Tima stood up. Four people were now resting on one end of the ladder. Lucky was flying back and forth between her and Matt as if to show her how *easy* it was. Tima knew everyone would hold the ladder secure . . . but pinned at just one end, it might shift beneath her as she got on. She lowered herself to her hands and knees and reached for the first rung beyond the edge of the ground. She took a steadying breath and then climbed onto the ladder. Its fine metal ridges dug into her hands and knees. She felt it tilt and caught her breath.

'Hang on! Wait!'

Uncle Fraser moved forward across three or four rungs, stretching out on his front beyond the ground, weighting the ladder with his upper body as far across the crevasse as he could safely reach. It did seem to help. Tima moved on. She tried not to look down but just couldn't help herself. The afternoon light was fading but she could make out that she was now suspended in thin air, above a drop as high as the average two-storey house. Maybe higher. The crevasse was V-shaped and filled with rocks; some tumbled to the bottom, others jutting out jaggedly like broken teeth. As she moved she could hear more rocks and stones falling, crunching, skittering, and pinging ever downward.

Stop looking, she told herself. *Move on! You're seconds away from getting into a nice warm car.* She moved on, but then another voice said: *What if the earth starts to shake NOW, eh? What then?* And it was almost as if she had dared the quake gods because at that point she caught a wisp of steam rising from the very bottom of the crevasse and everything began to tremble. She screamed and clung to the nearest rung, just as the pink and metallic gleam of a grub flashed by far down below. She could even hear its familiar, terrifying rumble. The aluminium ladder vibrated with it and some rocks on the upper ledges of the crevasse began to fall.

She heard the others shout out in alarm as the ladder behind her slewed sideways, tipping violently to her left. She wrapped her arms and legs around the rungs, clinging like a monkey as the others fought desperately to keep the bottom end anchored to the ground. But it was no good. The ladder was dropping. And she was dropping with it.

CHAPTER 34

Jamie always told people he couldn't remember the accident that had killed his parents and damaged him permanently. He'd been only three at the time, after all.

But this wasn't completely true. He believed he *did* remember something. It's just that it was almost impossible to describe. There was a colour . . . a dark red. And spirals of white. A sense of falling . . . that the world was tumbling past you like a river and leaving you behind forever. A desolate, desolate feeling.

This was as close as he could ever come to putting it into words, and even then it was only halfway there. He knew he would never truly be able to explain it . . . so he had never tried.

He hadn't ever expected to feel that unspeakable sensation again in his life. But he was feeling it now. As the ladder slid away beneath their arms and chests and chins and knees, and

Uncle Fraser flailed helplessly, tipping headfirst along with the metal strut and only just anchoring himself as Tima was tilted and twisted until she was clinging to the underside of the ladder, her hat falling off and disappearing into the jagged blackness . . . that desolate feeling was back.

He couldn't lose Tima. He *couldn't*. This was more than he could ever bear. The dropping end of the ladder snagged on a rock shelf and Tima was jolted brutally. Her knee lock was broken and now she was hanging by the crook of her elbow and her two bunched fists. Some kind of yodelling scream of horror was pouring out of his throat at the point he noticed the jagged blackness was *moving*. It was moving like *a cloud*—a cloud of black . . . rising. It looked like dense smoke but it wasn't moving like smoke . . . it had a kind of *purpose*. It wrapped itself around the ladder and then seemed to pool and hover just below the struggling girl. Jamie stared in utter wonder. Bats. They were *bats*. *Thousands* of black, glistening bats.

Tima stopped kicking. Her legs, lost in the blackness, seemed to rise and reconnect with the rungs. A moment later she was on top of the ladder, not under it. And then she was climbing. Fast. She shot up the rungs like a monkey, the black cloud dissolving away around her and spreading up into the sky as Elena sang out 'Thank you, thank you, *thank* you!'

Uncle Fraser grabbed Tima as soon as she was within reach and they all leaned back, weighting the ladder, while holding out their hands to help her to clamber up over his shoulders and onto firm ground. Then, with a groan, Uncle Fraser wrenched himself around from his upended position and managed, with help, to get back up too.

The second they released it, the ladder dropped with a shriek of stressed aluminium and plummeted, hissing and coughing, down into the crevasse. For a few seconds they all sat, panting, on the cold earth. The rumbling had stopped and an eerie quiet descended.

'Was that ... was that ...' murmured Uncle Fraser, '... a cloud of *bats?*'

'They—they must have been in a cave ... somewhere down there,' puffed Elena.

'They looked as if ...' he began.

'Can we get into the Jeep?' asked Matt. 'We're all really cold.'

'Jeep,' echoed Lucky, settling on his head. 'Really.'

Uncle Fraser stared at the starling and then glanced up at the sky.

'Did somebody just put the world into hyperdrive?' he said.

CHAPTER 35

'The first earthquake struck around 11.30 a.m. and there has been a series of localized tremors, some measuring 5.6 on the Richter scale, across the day.' Although the BBC newsreader was straight-faced and professional, there was a breathy disbelief about her delivery. 'But it's believed some deeper tremors may be responsible for three satellite masts coming down in the area, one of them blocking the A84 just north of Stirling for several hours. It's not yet known if anyone has died in what is an unprecedented natural disaster for Scotland.'

'They must have mended some of the satellite masts if we're getting telly,' said Uncle Fraser. 'Mobiles are still out, though.'

Images of helicopters hovering over mountains were relayed on screen as the presenter went on: 'Several remote villages have been cut off by broken mountain roads and the emergency services are reporting injuries—some severe—and a number of missing persons. The advice to people in the area is to stay indoors, but to get into doorways or under tables if a quake strikes again.'

Elena looked around the room. Everyone was wrapped up warmly in thick tartan blankets, drinking hot soup from mugs and dunking thickly-buttered chunks of bread, doled out to them by Jamie's granddad, Gregory. Everyone looked appalled ... as if they hadn't actually been *out* there, *experiencing* the earthquakes. Seeing it on the news was still shocking; especially how widely the quakes were occurring. Elena put her arm around Tima, on the sofa next to her. 'You OK?' she checked. She had been checking roughly every ten minutes for the past two hours.

Tima nudged her. 'I'm as OK as I was the last time you asked,' she said.

'I still can't believe what happened,' murmured Elena.

'We might have to call you Bat Girl,' said Tima, grinning and biting her soup-dipped bread. 'That was quite some rescue, calling up an entire colony!'

'They *were* amazing, I didn't even know if they could help but they just ... *lifted* you,' went on Elena, keeping her voice low. Jamie's uncle might have witnessed everything *she* had, but she suspected it was still better to let him believe Tima had somehow saved herself.

'I know,' said Tima. 'My big heavy human legs, lifted by bats! I guess there were a few thousand of them, working together, but ... wow.' She sighed. 'Good job none of the media choppers were passing by. Imagine my poor mum and dad watching *that* all over the News at Six!' Tima had called her parents as soon as they'd got back to the warm, well-kept crofters cottage where Jamie and his uncle and granddad lived, relieved to find their landline still working. Her mum and dad were thrilled to hear her voice and to know she was safe over in Jamie's family home. They seemed to accept Tima's explanation that she'd been out for an early dog walk with Jamie and Hamish and got stranded by a quake.

Elena had called her mum too. She'd been *mostly* honest.

'Mum? It's me.'

'Ellie! Are you OK?' Her mum sounded worried but not desperate, she was pleased to note.

'Yes . . . yes I'm fine. Can't talk for long because I've borrowed someone's phone. We're up in Scotland.'

'In Scotland? Of all the places! Have you see the news?!'

'Yes . . . yes I *have*. It's crazy! But we're safe. Having some soup, in fact.'

Mum had started asking more questions immediately, of course, but Elena had wound up the call quickly. 'Look, Mum—as soon as I'm home I'll explain it all to you, I promise.'

'When will you be home? What am I going to tell the school?' asked Mum.

'Tomorrow, I think,' said Elena. 'And it's still flu. Bye bye for now. Love you . . .'

Now, finishing her soup, Elena glanced over at Matt. 'Are you going to call your mum?' she asked, quietly. Matt shook his head.

'She'll be freaking out,' said Elena.

'Yeah—but if my dad picks up . . .'

'Just hang up,' said Elena. 'And block the caller ID before you dial.'

In the end Matt got up and, checking politely with Fraser and Gregory first, picked up the landline phone at the other side of the room. Elena watched as his rigid face melted into some kind of relief. She realized he must have got the answerphone. Straining her ears she heard him say: 'It's me. I'm OK. I'll be back soon. Don't worry.' Then he put down the receiver and stared at it for a few seconds before closing his eyes. She got up and went over to him. 'Matt—what are we going to do about the car? How can we get it back to Thornleigh when the road is broken?'

'Forget it. Nobody's going anywhere.'

Elena looked up to see Jamie's uncle, sitting at the old oak table in the kitchen end of the living area. 'Not until the aftershocks have stopped. Then we might head out and see what's happened to your car; find out if there's any direction it can be driven. It's an off-roader, yes?'

'A Land Rover,' said Matt.

'Good. I know all the off-road routes. There's a good chance I can get it back to a usable road. But for now, everyone needs to take it easy. Get some sleep here; we'll sort out a camp bed for you, Matt. Jamie will fit on the sofa. The g̲i̲ Jamie's bunk.'

'Thanks,' said Matt. He glanced at Elen was certain they were all thinking the same

This is not over. There is more we have to

CHAPTER 36

Jamie woke to the sound of whispering. He jerked up into a sitting position and Elena, Tima, and Matt glanced across at him, looking guilty. They were all geared up to go outside and—judging by their expressions—they hadn't been planning to take him along. He glanced at his watch. It was just before 11 p.m. Everyone had retired to bed, exhausted, at 9.30 p.m.—but clearly these guys had made a plan to get up and leave while he, Granddad, and Uncle Fraser were in dreamland.

'Where are you going?' he hissed. 'Without me?!' He felt a [s]betrayal.

[...]er to him, sitting on the end of the sofa.

[...]We don't mean to leave you out of things

[...]something about the grubs. And—'

[...]t Lurch coming along?' snapped Jamie,

as well as he *could* snap while not waking up his uncle and grandfather. 'Slowing you down. Getting in the way.'

They all looked shamefaced. 'We're just used to working together; the three of us,' explained Elena, quietly. 'We've been through stuff together, you know . . . and Tima didn't want to put you in any more danger.'

'Oh right, I see,' muttered Jamie, standing up. 'Yeah, of course. Go on without me. It'll be much easier that way. I guess you know your way around these mountains? You know all the paths and the hidden drops? Like the back of your hand?'

'He's got a point,' grunted Matt. 'He could be useful.'

'Of *course* he'll be useful,' said Tima. She picked up his coat from the peg by the door and gave it to him. 'Also, he did save my life down there.'

Jamie took his coat, shrugging. 'Well—you saved mine too,' he said.

He didn't find out what the plan was until they were all outside and walking. There was a bright three-quarter moon above them, painting the valley silvery white. They set out purposefully to the west, using torches to light their path. It took him a minute or two to realize they were being led . . . by a small, darkly-furred mammal which was leaping across the snow-dusted heather in undulating arcs and occasionally looking back to check on them through glinting dark eyes. Their guide had a bushy, blunt-ended tail with dark rings around it, flattened ears, and a striped coat. Jamie blinked and grabbed Tima's arm. 'Is that . . . a wildcat?'

'Yes,' said Tima. 'She's helping out.'

Jamie took a long breath. 'OK . . . and—where are we all going?' He was aware they were heading north-west, out in the opposite direction to the mountainside where he and Tima had entered the tunnels. Of course, they couldn't easily get back there with the crevasse in the way. He shivered, remembering Tima dangling above the drop.

'We need to get to the place where Vardof and his big brother were coming in and out,' said Tima. 'The place where the beam comes through.' She took a long breath of her own. 'This beam,' she said. 'It's the same one that gave us our Night Speakers talents.'

'Uhuh,' said Jamie, puffing a little as they scrambled up a sharp incline, the wildcat bobbing away at the front.

'We had it explained to us once by someone who knows all about it,' went on Tima. 'Someone opened up this kind of wormhole between planets—here in the Highlands—using this energy beam which flows back and forth between different dimensions. There's one in Thornleigh, too, where we live. The two are connected.'

'OK,' said Jamie. 'So . . . this magical beam. You know where to find it?'

'We don't,' said Tima. 'But they do.'

Jamie realized the wildcat had been joined by several owls, flying silently in loops above.

'So—we find this cave with the beam and then what? Vardof and his brother left hours ago. The grubs have been left behind—that's what you said. We're too late.'

'We might not be,' said Tima. 'I heard Vardof's brother

saying the meteor storm was going to hit in the next twenty-four hours, and that was at about midday. So . . . they might still be loading up on this moon. Maybe we can follow them through the corridor and catch up with them.'

'And then what? Ask them nicely to come back for their pets?'

Elena and Matt paused to look back. 'We don't know yet,' said Elena. 'We just know we have to try *something*. So . . . we're getting ourselves there and working it out as we go along.'

Jamie thought it was a pretty thin plan. He didn't say so, though. Partly because he couldn't think of a better one, and partly because at this point, the ground opened up and swallowed them all.

CHAPTER 37

Afterwards, as he regained his senses, Matt realized Lucky and the owls had tried to warn them. At the point he and Elena had turned back to talk to Tima and Jamie, the birds had risen higher and sent out a distress call to each other and to their human party.

But the falling away of the mountainside was so abrupt there was nothing any of them could have done. The thundering in his ears, coupled with the sudden drop and the sting of flying grit, took his breath away. The hard landing almost stopped it. He lay with his head downwards, feeling something warm trickling from his jaw to his ear and a stinging bolt of pain through the bandaged wound in his upper arm. The rumbling had abated and now he could hear his own ragged breathing and a high-pitched cry. Something scratched his face.

Lucky. She had just landed on his chin and was staring down at him, her beady dark eyes shining with what certainly looked like concern. Matt realized he could see Lucky well. They were bathed in light. He carefully tried out his limbs and his spine and found they could move. He was sore . . . but not broken. Beneath him was a mattress of heather. The whole mountainside had crumpled inward, but the thickly-woven surface of springy vegetation had probably saved his life.

He sat up carefully, saw Elena and Tima nearby, also dazed, but moving. Behind them, Jamie was up on his knees, staring across Matt's shoulder with a rigid expression. Matt turned and looked. There was the source of the light. A massive circular edifice of metal teeth and a lone white eye—like the headlamp on an old locomotive. Matt gulped. This was it. A mining grub. It must have just mined this passage and caused the collapse. Looking up, he could see the night sky not too far above—it looked as if they had only fallen three or four metres. The wildcat stared down at them from the edge of the drop, looking bewildered.

'Is it going to kill us?' Elena breathed, now sitting up and staring across at the grub.

Tima got shakily to her feet. 'I don't know,' she said. 'I don't think so. I mean . . . they're not aggressive. They just do as they're told.'

'But there's nobody here to tell them what to do,' pointed out Matt. 'So . . . what *do* they do?'

'They just keep moving,' said Tima, walking towards the grub. In its pale light Matt could see Tima was scratched and bruised. Her face was a picture of brave determination, though. She was going to communicate with the grub. Well, he decided, she wasn't going to do it alone. He got up too, wincing as a stab of pain went through his left leg. He hobbled after Tima.

Elena glanced up at the wildcat. 'It's OK,' she said. 'We'll be all right.' As the creature slipped away she joined Matt and Tima by the grub. Jamie scrambled to his feet and caught up with them.

The tunnel they were in was wider than the grub that had made it. It seemed to be double the width. The grub, as they drew closer, did not move, although there was space enough around the collapse for it to do so. Its fearsome wheels of teeth remained still, but the flesh inside its metal exoskeleton was rising and falling. Instinctively, the Night Speakers moved to its flank and touched their hands tentatively to the skin between the metal rings. It was warm. Matt felt the creature's pulse, slow and steady and then speeding up as first Tima and then he and Elena tilted in and rested their foreheads against it. The conversation was slow at first. It was impossible to tell which of them was speaking; connected through the grub's skin and nervous system, they seemed to speak as one.

We don't want to hurt you.

Hurt.

No. We don't want to.

No.

We need to find Vardof.

Need.

We need to get you all away from these mountains. You're

destroying them. Killing animals. Killing people, maybe, too.

Away.

Yes. Away. Back through the corridor. Through the beam.

The beam. (The creature seemed to sigh, contentedly.)

Do you know where the beam comes in?

Know.

Can you take us there?

Take.

Suddenly the creature was thrumming. Then it was rumbling and giving off an odd, wheezy whistle. They all jerked their heads away from its side.

'The footplate!' yelled Tima. 'Quick!'

She ran towards the back of the grub and Matt was astonished to see there *was* a metal platform attached to the rear end—with a curved safety rail at about hip height, just as Jamie had described it. 'Come on!' yelled Tima. 'We're hitching a lift!'

Jamie broke into an awkward run as they all scrambled onto the footplate, ducking under the rail and stepping up, and for one horrible moment it looked as if he might be left behind. The grub began to move—fast—before he reached them. Jamie's uneven gallop sped up and he flung himself forward, arms outstretched. Matt grabbed him and hauled him onto the rail, just as the grub went up a gear and began to *thunder* along the tunnel. Jamie's legs flapped in the air as Matt, Elena, and Tima dragged him over and onto the footplate. Lucky flew in at the last moment and tucked herself onto Matt's shoulder, close against his neck, her tiny feathered body thrumming with fear.

There was barely enough space for them all so they clung

tightly to each other, as well as the guard rail, and watched, open-mouthed, as the smooth, wide tunnel closed down to a smooth, narrow tunnel and then flashed into a wide cavern and then another narrow tunnel, twisting and turning, rising and falling. For Matt it was not unlike travelling by tube train in London—and every bit as crowded.

He was terrified but thrilled. The speed was breathtaking. He briefly wondered what might happen if another grub was thundering along in the opposite direction. A head-on collision would be carnage. 'I hope it knows where it's going!' he shouted, over the rumble of the grub's hundreds of feet.

Tima turned and peered up at him from where she was squeezed in under his right armpit. 'It does. It's taking us to the beam, Matt! It's taking us to the beam!'

A fizz of disbelief ran through him. He'd spent so many nights wandering the hillsides in Thornleigh, hoping to find an entrance to the cave where the beam came through, all in vain. He'd never imagined he'd find a path to it four hundred miles north! Could this *really* be the way in? On the back of a rock-eating alien cyborg worm?

They saw other grubs. Some were waiting in clusters in larger caverns, almost like a herd. Others were sharing the larger tunnels. These grubs zoomed past with a crack of displaced air, like an Intercity-Express. 'Keep your hands and feet well inside!' yelled Matt. 'And don't look around towards the front.' It was dumb advice. Everyone had worked out that they could lose a limb—or their head—if they leaned out beyond the grub's back end.

'They have a kind of radar,' said Tima, who was pressing one hand onto the grub's huge rump and working hard on getting into its simple mind. 'They know where all the others are. So they never crash into another one—WOAH!'

The grub tilted sharply to the left as it took a long, wide bend, and they all hung on for dear life. Matt wondered if they ought to ask it to slow down a bit—but then rejected the idea as soon as the creature righted itself on a long, straight stretch. How far had they travelled by now? Two kilometres? Five? Ten? Maybe double that. In the tunnels it was impossible to tell what speed they were going. Now the creature was going downhill. Steeply downhill. They were all tipped against its rear end, reclining uneasily at what must have been a forty-five degree angle. Matt could also sense the creature slowing down; putting its brakes on. The momentum dropped and the grub's path smoothly flattened out, allowing them all to stand upright again.

Matt realized he'd been holding his breath, and let out a long exhalation. He needed to find some *workable* level of panic . . . this might be a long ride.

It *was* a long ride. At least half an hour passed, during which they all stayed close, watching this subterranean world flash by until, at last, their conveyance began to ease down a few gears and adopt a steadier pace. As they slowed Matt saw the smooth curved walls of the tunnel closing tightly once more; he was sure there were seams of gold and pale white crystal flashing by he and there, highlighted by the glow shed by the grub as it pass

'We're nearly here,' whispered Elena. 'Can you feel i

'What time is it?' asked Tima.

Matt looked at his watch. He gulped. 'It's twelve thirty-four,' he said. Back in Thornleigh, the beam would be passing through their bedrooms right now. Something of the joyous tingle he felt whenever it happened was around him at that moment . . . not so intense but still washing over him, making goosebumps sweep across his neck and shoulders. Just imagining it, he guessed, was enough.

The grub was taking another curve, at walking pace. There was a blue light from somewhere, mixing with the grub's own pink-white gleam. The rock walls lifted and dropped, undulating and natural—there was no evidence of mined tunnels here. The grub stopped. It gave a long, whistling sigh and then powered down.

'Do we go on alone from here?' asked Tima, her palm still pressed to its skin.

Matt felt and heard the grub in his head: *Go on*.

On shaky legs he stepped down onto the solid floor of the small cave, and then turned to help Jamie as Elena and Tima leapt down easily. Jamie staggered slightly and Matt reminded himself that the boy had not shared the life and death experiences he and Elena and Tima had over the past year. He was probably freaking out.

'You OK?' he said, gripping Jamie's shoulders.

'That . . .' said Jamie, puffing slightly, '. . . was the best ride of LIFE!'

Matt grinned and slapped the boy's back. 'Correct answer!'

He turned to see Tima and Elena watching him and then owards a tight turn in the passage, past some solid rippling curtains of what must be limestone, he guessed. The light diffusing past this formation was fizzing and sparkling.

It was unmistakable.

Matt felt his throat tighten and his heartbeat thud faster.

This was beam light.

CHAPTER 38

The cave wasn't huge; maybe the size of a small house. It was domed, its ceiling curving upwards and tapering to a fine chimney in the centre. Its walls gently sparkled. But Tima had no more than a moment to take in details—her eyes were fixed on a small, hexagonal plinth, with a small, hexagonal post in the centre, not much bigger than a stick of chalk. Out of the post, in a straight golden line, shone the beam.

It travelled at an almost ninety degree angle, slanting down slightly and flowing directly into the opposite wall of the cave . . . and it was simply beautiful. The golden light within it was moving; flowing and bubbling and sparkling with other colours too. The song it sang brought the same lump to her throat as it always did, when the pulse of the beam reached them, 400 miles to the south-east, shooting on through to its destination somewhere inside the hills around Thornleigh.

They stood and stared. Wondered. Tried to clear their minds and make a decision . . . then just stood and stared some more. Tima could sense that Elena and Matt were in exactly the same state as she was.

'That is so beautiful.'

Tima jolted and turned, remembering that Jamie was with them.

'Is this it?' he said. 'Is it your beam? Does it know you?'

As if it had somehow heard him, the beam suddenly sent out spinning golden-pink specks around the room, like a dandelion clock of light. Some of them found the Night Speakers and connected to them, prickling across their faces. The sensation was almost unbearably wonderful; Tima heard herself cry out.

It was Jamie who finally spoke. 'Look—we need you to help us,' he said, staring at the post amid the sparkling darts of gold. 'Are you still connected to the other place . . . to the moon . . . the place the mining grubs came from?'

The beam did not speak, exactly, but something in its note changed . . . a low vibration came through . . . and another kind of light began to intensify. This second beam was pale green and rose in a vertical column, vanishing into the tapering chimney of the cave ceiling. Held in the tingling embrace of the beam's dandelion clock, the Night Speakers all took a deep breath and let it out again, shakily.

'So . . . now what?' asked Jamie.

The Night Speakers looked at each other. *Fair point,*

thought Tima. *Now what, indeed?'* She felt a little stupefied. She didn't really want to move. To be touched by the beam felt so wonderful. She could very possibly stay here, just like this, forever.

'It's probably a bit like a teleport beam, you know, like in Star Trek,' Jamie was saying. 'It's energy, isn't it? You step into it and—vooom—off you go!' He stepped towards the hexagonal plinth, the light dancing in his eyes. 'You're just particles,' he went on. 'I saw a science thing on telly once . . . they called it . . . *quantum entanglement.* Great name for a band; that's what I thought. Never thought it could really work. But those grubs . . . they must have been quantum entangled to get here. So . . . here goes.'

Tima broke out of her stupor too late to stop him as he stepped onto the plinth and put his hand into the green light. She screamed: 'JAMIE, NO!' and leapt across the cave floor to grab him.

But Jamie was just particles.

CHAPTER 39

Jamie felt as if ants made of ice were crawling over his entire body. He couldn't scream. He couldn't move. Too late he realized he'd been reckless and stupid. He had asked this beam post thing to show him the corridor to another dimension and it had done exactly that. Then he'd just stepped into it without considering the small issue of whether he would be able to EXIST in that dimension.

Just before he lost consciousness he heard someone shout and a felt a thud on his chest.

The next thing he knew, he was lying flat on his back on the floor of the beam cave, with Tima staring down at him in horror. A familiar gruff voice said: 'I thought you two were dead! How did you get away from the grubs?'

Jamie faded out for a while and then felt someone gently

slapping his face. 'Jamie—come on—wake up!' It was Tima. Behind her he could make out Matt and Elena, pressed against the cave wall, their hands raised.

The familiar voice was back. It was Vardof. 'I don't have to do *anything*,' he was saying, waving some kind of flashing red weapon while Matt glowered at him. 'You're lucky I brought this one back. If I hadn't seen him coming through he'd be a cloud of atoms by now. What did you think you were *doing*?' he shouted, turning to glare at Jamie.

'Please,' grunted Jamie, sitting up slowly. 'You have to help us before you go. You have to take the grubs with you. They're causing earthquakes all over the place. The mountains are falling in.'

'I haven't got time,' hissed Vardof. 'I should already be off that moon. My brother's not going to wait much longer, you know. We were just about to take off.'

'We heard you say something back in the tunnels,' said Tima. 'Something about . . . prop fungus?'

Vardof looked a little sheepish and scratched his nose with the end of the flashing red weapon. 'Oh . . . that. Yeah. I should've used prop fungus but I didn't know. It stops the tunnels falling in. Too late now though.'

'It's *not* too late!' said Tima, getting up and grabbing his free arm. 'Just give it to us and *we* can do it. We can prop up the tunnels.'

Vardof considered this for a moment and then shook his head. 'It won't work. I mean, yeah, you could get the grubs to spray it around for you but it'll run out eventually . . . and the grubs won't. They'll just keep eating the rock, making new tunnels. They don't know how to stop.'

Tima, ignoring his laser gun or whatever it was, went to him and put her hand on his free arm. 'Vardof . . . you're not like your brother,' she said, gazing up into his whiskery face. 'I know that you . . . *care*. There must be *something* you can do.'

Vardof screwed up his eyes and shook his head for several seconds, as if he were having a ferocious argument with himself. Then he turned, stepped into the green shaft of light, and vanished. The shaft vanished too, a second later.

There was a long silence.

'Well, that's that, then,' said Tima. She turned to look at Jamie. 'I'm so sorry. I really thought we could—GAH!' A burst of energy rocked the cave and they were all knocked off their feet as green light swept the chamber again. On the floor was a large metallic case. And standing on it, see-through and flickering, was a hologram of Vardof.

'Shut up and listen,' he said. 'I've only got sixty seconds before my brother flies off this rock without me.'

They all gaped at him. 'Go on!' urged Jamie.

'In this case is the prop fungus. You attach it to the grubs and let them go. They know what to do. They'll sort out all the tunnels.'

'OK—and then what?' asked Matt.

'SHUT UP! FORTY seconds left!' yelled Vardof. 'I've put in another beam post at this end—on this moon. It'll take the grubs into a cavern under the surface—away from the meteor storm so they won't get pulped. But you need to get them through fast. It's a temporary beam post. It won't last more than three Earth hours once I'm gone. Get them all over before it times out. Leave any behind on Earth and it's your problem, not mine.'

The holographic man looked anxiously over his shoulder and then back towards Tima. 'I never wanted to kill you,' he said. 'Sorry. Good luck.'

They just had time to see him turn and run before the hologram vanished.

CHAPTER 40

'OK,' said Jamie. 'We've got work to do.' He crouched over the case. It was big enough to accommodate Tima, if she curled up like a cat. He felt around some buttons on its side and then, with a sudden buzz, the top of it sprang open. Inside were hundreds of small metal canisters, tightly packed together.

'Prop fungus,' said Tima. 'We need to get all the grubs together and we need to load these onto them.'

Jamie nodded over at the grub they'd travelled on. A sliver of its scary teeth-laden face was just visible beyond a curtain of stalactites at the far end of the cave. 'Let's see where these things go.'

Tima plucked one of the canisters into her palm. It shone like silver and had a dull red waxy seal at the top end. They all trooped to the far end of the grub where Jamie crouched down, trying to find a place to load the canister.

'There's probably a hole or an indent . . . somewhere it attaches,' Matt said.

Tima crouched down too.

'Wait,' said Elena. 'Did you see that?'

'What?' they all chorused.

'A little flicker of blue light . . . right there . . .' Elena pointed to the mid-point underside of the footplate. 'Tima—wave the canister here.' Tima did and the flicker of light became a blue glow and they saw a semicircle of metal, a bit like a cupholder in a car, emerge smoothly from it. Tima pushed the canister into it until it clicked and the whole thing lit up blue.

Then they stood and looked at it, expectantly.

Two minutes later, nothing else had happened.

'How do we get it to work?' asked Elena, finally. 'And how are we going to get them all to come to us and get one attached?'

Tima climbed up on the footplate and pressed her palms and her forehead to the skin of the grub. *What do we do?* she asked. *We need you to travel the tunnels and put this prop fungus stuff all over the walls . . . make them safe. Can you do that?*

The response she got back was positive. Yes. The grub could do that. But it wasn't doing it. It wasn't doing anything. Tima got back down where the others were all looking at her, hoping she'd worked it all out. 'I don't know,' she said, suddenly feeling overwhelmed by tiredness. 'It's not arguing with me—it's happy to do as we ask. But . . . it seems to be waiting for something. A special word? A signal? I don't know.'

Jamie suddenly gave a shout and pulled something away

from the inside of the case lid—a dark blue hexagonal thing. It was about the size of a dinner plate and had several buttons around its rim. It looked, thought Tima as she peered over his shoulder, like a retro handheld computer game.

Jamie prodded a button and the hexagon filled with pinpricks of white light. Some were moving, some were still, and one solitary light, right in the centre, was green. Right beside the green was an orange light.

'What is it?' asked Matt. 'What does it mean?'

'I think . . . it's a map,' said Jamie. 'Like a satnav. I think these white lights are all the grubs. You can see them moving around.'

Elena knelt down and scrutinized the screen. 'You're right,' she said. 'You can tell by the movements. And look—that green light in the middle—I think that's the green beam Jamie just went through. It's still there, waiting. This orange light must be where *we* are now. And here's our grub.' She pointed to a stationary white light close to the orange.

'But there can only be about twenty white lights here,' said Matt, tapping the screen. 'And didn't you say there are ninety or so grubs in the mountains?'

'Yes,' said Tima.

'Wait,' said Jamie. 'This is a close-up view.' His fingers moved to another button and it slid smoothly along the edge of the console like a fader. The view shifted; the lights became tinier and more numerous. It was exactly like pulling out the view of a satnav map.

Along one edge of the screen there were figures of some

kind, in a column, each swiftly changing. 'I think these must be numbers,' Elena said. 'Or I suppose they could be letters . . . but I don't recognize them. Do you?' The others shook their heads.

'I thought you could understand any language,' said Jamie.

'We need to *hear* it,' said Matt. 'Reading isn't the same. It's an ear thing. Anyway, it doesn't matter. We can work out what this is. It's a map of the grubs and where they are. Now we need to work out how to call them back to us so we can set up this fungus stuff and get them to run around the tunnels like underground crop-spraying machines.'

'There isn't room to call them all to us here, anyway,' pointed out Elena. 'I think we need to go back to one of the big chambers and call them there. Come on. Let's get back on the footplate. We can ask the grub to take us back and try to work out the console as we go.'

They hefted the case onto the footplate and then all clambered up, sitting on it as Tima stood and connected with the grub again. Happily the grub seemed fine to go with her request simply to return to the nearest big chamber. It reversed up the passage, found a little extra space and turned tightly in it. Then, thrumming up its engines . . . or its organic heart . . . or probably both, it began to move gently along until it entered the circular tunnel. Tima wondered why it wasn't picking up speed. Then the answer came with a gentle pop.

'The canister!' yelled Matt. 'It just opened!'

Tima twisted around to look behind her and saw a filmy spray rise up from the back of the footplate. Of course—they had been in a natural part of the caves until now. That part hadn't *needed* any prop fungus. The spray shimmered with a faint rainbow haze and began to fan out across the walls and ceiling of the tunnel.

'Don't breathe it in!' warned Elena, covering her mouth and nose. 'It's a fungus. We have no idea what it might do to us.'

But the grub was picking up speed now and the spray of fine spores was left in their wake; Tima couldn't detect any of it on her skin or in her nostrils.

'I think I might have found out something,' Jamie said, still leaning over the console and hanging on to the rail as their grub bus began to speed up. The map showed the green light edging away to one side and the orange light remaining in the centre of the screen, partly merged with a white light. 'So, this orange light is us . . . or the satnav itself,' he said. 'Riding on the grub. And look now.' He pressed a button and a ring of blue arrows appeared across the screen. They were pointing inwards towards the central orange light and pulsing.

'What does that mean?' asked Tima.

They reached one of the huge chambers at that moment. 'I think we're about to find out,' said Jamie.

As they emerged from the tunnel and rolled to a halt in the centre of a vast cavern they were left in no doubt. At least ten mining grubs came into view—all heading directly for them. It was a terrifying sight. Their massive spinning teeth faces were moving slowly, as if gently revving up for some serious human pulping.

'It's OK,' said Tima, trying to keep the shake out of her voice. 'They're just coming to see our grub . . . it's communicating with them.'

'Or they're responding to *this*,' said Jamie—pointing to the console and the inward-moving arrows.

Their grub came to a halt in the centre of the chamber and they watched the others get closer. Tima held her breath and let it out in a long, relieved sigh as the other grubs came to a stop. 'Right,' said Matt, springing up. 'Time to load up all these fungus babies!'

Everyone stepped down onto the cave floor with wary glances at the crowd of alien creatures. The grubs stood, spinning teeth now motionless, staring back through their single headlamp eyes, faintly hissing and sending out a thin grey vapour from somewhere within their many caterpillar legs.

'Will they be OK with this?' asked Matt, as they opened the case and took out a canister each. 'They're not going to suddenly freak out and mince us if we start messing with their backsides, are they? Can you just check again, Tima?'

Tima leant her forehead between the rings of metal, connecting with the grub's fleshy side. *Are they all OK with us loading the canisters?* she asked. She stood upright again. 'It's fine. This is what their keepers do all the time. They're just responding as if we're their keepers. Honestly . . . they're no more dangerous than a herd of cows.'

'Yeah. Cows that can drill a massive hole right through you,' added Jamie. 'If they're in the mood. Still—we've got no choice. We have to make these tunnels safe.'

The ground beneath them rumbled and shuddered, illustrating Jamie's last point. They all stood stock-still, glancing at each other fearfully, but after a few seconds the rumbling stopped. Tima glanced up, expecting to see a great big crack running across the ceiling of the cave. There wasn't one. They were safe . . . for now.

It took them a few minutes to attach the canisters to every grub in the chamber. Several more arrived and squeezed in as they worked, and they loaded those too. Then Tima asked their grub to communicate with the others, explaining that they must revisit all their tunnels, spray them all with prop fungus—and then come back to the main chamber.

'They get it,' she said to Matt. 'They're going to do it.'

'OK—so that's fifteen of them,' said Matt as the cavern emptied with a chorus of rumbles, whistles, and steamy hisses. 'So . . . what about all the others?'

'They're coming.' Jamie held up the console. At the edge the arrows were still pulsing—and the white dots were steadily heading for their orange dot, some of them forming long lines; queuing along the tunnels they had made.

'Great,' said Matt, nodding. 'So . . . all we've got to do is load them all up, send them out to spray fungus everywhere . . . then get them back . . . then take them all to the beam cave and teleport them to an alien moon!'

Elena grinned. 'Easy!'

CHAPTER 41

It seemed to be going fine. Like clockwork. On Jamie's hexagon of alien tech they could see the little dots moving around as the grubs sprayed the prop fungus. Matt asked to take a look at it and Jamie shrugged and handed it over. Matt examined it closely and then twisted a button on the side of the console. He let out a shout: 'Woah, that's better. Look!' Lucky, perched on his woollen hat, peered down too. Elena and Tima joined them, staring down at the screen.

It was now showing a network of tunnels, marked out in pale pink. As they watched, they noticed the tunnels behind some of the travelling dots changing colour—to pale blue. 'I think it's showing us which tunnels have been fungus-propped!' said Matt, grinning excitedly as if he'd just got a brand new game. He zoomed out and they saw what must have been miles of tunnels, spreading in a rough crescent across the map.

Jamie shook off annoyance with himself for not discovering the fungus-spreading map before Matt did. 'They're moving fast,' he said, checking his watch. 'We've got just over two hours. I think we can do it.'

'They're all coming right back here as soon as they've finished propping their tunnels,' said Tima. 'So as soon as they do, we can start riding them back to the beam cave and sending them home to their lovely, cosy, tasty moon. We can do this.' She raised a palm for Jamie to high five. It took him a while to give her five back. She kindly kept her palm in place until he got there.

The grub they'd first connected with stayed put with them in what now resembled a bus station at rush hour. It seemed to be communicating with all the rest like a queen bee in a hive, so Tima named it Queenie.

When two grubs arrived back with prop fungus canisters already in place, their seals blown, Jamie called over to Tima. 'I think these guys are done.' He picked out a canister and shook it. 'It's empty.'

'OK, Queenie,' said Tima, stroking their grub's skin. 'Have they finished?'

Jamie, Elena, and Matt watched, tense with hope.

'Yes—they've propped all their tunnels!' she told them. She grinned, turned back to the grub and continued. 'So we need to get these guys back to the beam cave and into the green light so they can go to their new home.' Jamie saw the grub shiver at the mention of the beam.

'Do you know how to get them through?' Elena asked Jamie, while Matt went back to fiddling with the hexagonal console, tracking the progress of all the other grubs. 'I mean . . . you went inside it, didn't you?'

Jamie glanced around at them all. 'I think they just go inside it, like I did. Only . . . *they* won't come bouncing out again on their bums. I hope.'

Matt stood up. 'OK—I think me and Elena should keep loading them up and sending them out with the prop fungus . . . and Jamie and Tima should be in charge of getting the grubs home as soon as they come back from propping. We've got . . .' he glanced at the console, 'quite a lot left to do. There are actually ninety-seven in total, including Queenie.'

'How do you know?' asked Tima.

'I've been counting . . . and tracking them,' said Matt. 'It's no big deal. It's a lot easier than most Xbox games.'

Jamie and Tima climbed on board Queenie and they moved away in convoy with the other two behind them. Jamie still felt a shudder run through him as those circles of teeth followed them, just a car's length away from where they rode the footplate. He believed Tima when she said they were just like a herd of cows but even cows had their moments.

'Look . . .' Tima cried, waving around them. The tunnel walls and ceilings were glittering with rainbow colours in a pattern of swoops and curves, almost like fish scales. 'It must be the fungus! It's beautiful!'

'As long as it's strong,' said Jamie, 'I don't care *what* it looks like.'

The grub convoy sped up again but now they knew what to look for they saw more and more of the glittering scales and Jamie began to feel some sense of hope that all this effort might just make a difference.

They reached the beam cave in minutes and Queenie pulled over to the side of the tunnel to allow Jamie and Tima to alight and lead the other two past her.

Back in the cave the seeds of pink light were still dancing and the vertical green shaft continued to thrum gently. Jamie and Tima stood back and waved the first grub towards it. The creature paused for a moment, as if uncertain. Tima gently patted its flank. 'It's OK. You're going home now!'

The creature let out what sounded like a sigh and then trundled forward into the green shaft, disappearing into it like a train entering a tunnel. It was the biggest, most mind-bending magic trick Jamie had ever seen.

The second grub needed no encouragement. It gave a short whistle and followed its friend.

Jamie held up his hand and Tima high fived *him* much more efficiently.

'Let's go and get some more!' said Tima, grinning. They rode Queenie back again even more quickly and arrived back in Grub Central Station to find several more waiting.

'It worked!' Tima yelled, jumping off the footplate and punching the air. 'Get IN!'

'Good. Only ninety-five left to do,' said Elena, attaching another canister and actually patting the rump of the grub to send it on its way.

Jamie and Tima worked out they could take five grubs with them on the next run; there was just enough space to manoeuvre them around before sending them on. Over the next hour they took 14 trips and evacuated a further 70 grubs.

'Twenty-five left,' said Jamie as they arrived back from the latest run. 'They must have done all their propping by now.'

'Um,' said Elena, and Jamie could see at once that something was wrong. Elena and Matt were both staring at the console. 'Come and see this,' said Elena, quietly.

Matt held out the screen, zoomed out to take in the entire threadlike network of tunnels. Around twenty white lights were heading back to them, along blue tunnels. The problem looked tiny. Just a few lines of pale pink—unpropped tunnels. And two dots in those tunnels . . . motionless.

'What's up with *them*?' asked Jamie, feeling a cold pinch in his chest.

'They haven't moved for the whole time I've been looking,' said Matt. 'I think they're trapped—probably behind a rockfall from one of the earthquakes.'

'But they *eat* rock!' said Jamie. 'Why aren't they just drilling through it with their teeth?'

'We don't know,' said Matt. 'But there's something else.'

Matt prodded another button and certain areas of the screen began to flash in circular pulses of red. 'I think these show seismic activity,' he said. 'Quakes and tremors. I found them earlier, all over the place—but as the tunnels turned blue, any red flashing stopped in those areas. This bit over here—where these two last grubs are—it's the only unstable part left.'

'We need to get there,' said Jamie. 'We need to take the canisters with us—get through to them and get them to prop those tunnels right now! It could all come down any time.'

'Wait,' said Tima. 'I think . . . I think I might know why they've stopped.' She went to Queenie, who was in standby mode, teeth motionless, and pressed her forehead against the creature's glowing white eye. She looked up after a few seconds. 'They're not moving,' she said, 'because Queenie has told them not to.'

'Why?!' demanded Jamie.

'I think it's because the whole area will fall in if they try to burrow through the rockfall. Queenie knows what we're doing. She's trying to help.'

'So . . . if they can't come to us,' said Elena. 'We have to go to them.'

CHAPTER 42

'Does it know where to go?' shouted Elena, gripping the handrail as her hair blew around her face.

'Yes, she does,' yelled back Tima, hanging on tightly next to her. 'They're all connected, you know—like bees and ants. I've asked her to find the quake zone and the last two grubs. She knows where she's going.'

'Good—aaaargh!' squeaked Elena as the grub turned a tight corner at incredibly high speed. She was relieved Jamie had agreed to stay behind with Matt and get the last of the other grubs home. He would have found it very hard to hold on for this ride.

They shot down the tunnel, through another rocky chamber and then had to hang on for dear life as Queenie suddenly veered up at an alarming tilt, skirting the edge of a bubbling pool of water, as wide as a basketball court. Her light picked out the slowly spinning body of another grub, drowned and floating on its side. Elena felt a spasm of grief go through Queenie's mind. She pressed a hand to the creature's skin and sent in: *I'm so sorry about your friend.* Something came back . . . a kind of appreciation 'Are you getting this?' she asked Tima, who was also in close contact with Queenie's skin.

Tima nodded. 'They feel everything we feel. People are always making out that invertebrates are just like machines. Well they're not. This is the biggest, scariest invertebrate I've ever met—but she cares about her family. She even cares about *us.*'

Elena shrieked and ducked sideways as a large lump of rock fell from the ceiling and rebounded off the handrail. More rocks followed as the grub thundered back into a tunnel.

'Are you OK?' shouted Tima, her eyes wide with fright.

'We must be close—we're in the quake zone!' Elena called back.

There was a hiss and suddenly the prop fungus began spraying behind them. Queenie was doing her best to make it safer.

Then they emerged into another chamber and this one was filled with early morning light—a massive crack rose in the rock above them, shafts of pale winter sun lighting the boulder-strewn collapse beneath. The grub slowed down and stopped beneath the open roof, in front of a pile of fallen rock.

'I think we're close,' said Elena. 'We need to go up and look—check we're in the right place.'

'What now?' said Tima, getting off the footplate and

going around to address Queenie face-to-face. The grub's teeth suddenly began to spin and Tima took a step backwards.

'Careful!' warned Elena.

'It's OK,' said Tima. 'She's going to burrow through to them . . . slowly.'

They stood, waiting while the creature churned slowly through the rock. Loose stone began to fly in all directions. Grit hit them in the face several times. 'I think we should get up out of the way a bit,' suggested Elena. 'Climb up there, maybe. It looks quite stable.'

The slope was surprisingly solid and unmoving and, having climbed halfway up, out of reach of flying grit, Elena got the urge to keep going, to remind herself what the outside world looked like. She reached up and hauled herself over a craggy bit of granite crowned with icy grass. 'Come and see, Tima,' she called back. 'Queenie's going to be ages yet.'

They were on a steep slope, overlooking a valley with a cluster of dwellings about half a kilometre away above a flat grey loch. Elena might have mistaken it for the place where she and Matt had rescued Agnes but the loch was a different shape. Tima began to climb up to her. Elena felt movement and saw a vole sitting on her boot. It stayed quite still, looking up at her, tiny whiskers twitching.

Tima arrived, clambering out and standing next to her. 'That's Loch View!' she said. 'That's where Mum and Dad are!'

Elena did not reply. She stared down at the vole. Then she reached down and collected it in her palm, just as another of those quakes began to roll across the glen. Tima shrieked and grabbed her arm. 'Get down!'

They both hit the ground, Elena still holding the vole aloft in one palm. 'It's not here,' she said. 'We're OK here.'

'Where . . . where *is* it?' asked Tima and Elena guessed she might already be picking up the news from the vole . . . or maybe from insects.

Elena pointed to the dwellings above the loch. 'It's there.'

Tima shot back up onto her feet and began to run down the slope, stumbling, picking herself up, running on.

'Tima! Waaaaait!' Elena ran after her. 'It's not safe down there!'

'My mum and dad are down there!' yelled Tima. 'I have to warn them! I have to get them out of there!'

Elena glanced back down at Queenie, who was halfway through the rockfall and still going slow. She groaned and took off after her friend.

'We've got to move them over THERE!' Tima yelled back as she pelted on down the slope. 'To the other side of the loch! There are no tunnels over there. We've got to get the people over there. NOW! Elena . . . call them. Call all your mammals. My insects . . . they can't help now. There aren't enough of them and they can't show the way.'

Elena, scrambling down behind, yelled: 'OK. I've got this.' Even as she said it, several deer were running up the mountainside towards them. They swerved as she pointed them back towards the loch but one, the stag from yesterday, she was sure, made straight for Tima.

'TIMA!' bawled Elena. 'Get on! Get ON! You've got a lift!'

Tima turned, ran up a jutting lump of rock and then threw herself onto the back of the stag. Thank god Tima was a posh girl who went horse riding, thought Elena. She had some idea what to do . . . Elena wished she could jump on another stag and race after them but she knew she was too heavy. A stag's spine wasn't cut out for human riders—but it could bear the weight of someone small and slight like Tima for a while.

All she could do was run after Tima and the herd—and *will* every other mammal in the valley to run with them to make it clear to the people in the village where the safe spot was.

But as the earth shook under her feet and she was pitched forward, getting a face full of heather, she wondered if they were too late.

CHAPTER 43

The exodus had begun even before they reached the holiday park. As she rode down, Tima could feel and see the movement around her. Across the peaks and folds of the land everything was travelling. Deer, foxes, rabbits, mice, voles, wildcats . . . even otters. A living stream of mammals was making for the holiday village.

The animals were following their own instinct as much as any plea from Elena. They did not run *through* the holiday park, sensing it could collapse into the mountain at any time. Instead, they skirted past it and ran on down to the loch and around its western end, heading for the safety of the far side.

Clinging on to the stag with her arms around its neck and her knees tight to its flanks, Tima's throat was seized up with fear as they fled down past the perimeter fence with all its twinkling fairy lights. What if they were too late? The earth kept quaking. As they got closer she could make out a knot of people, huddled in the centre of the tiny village. And as they got closer still there was a massive rumble and one of the lodges tilted erratically sideways. The hot tub on its deck tipped over and water sprang out of it in a frothy torrent.

She heard someone scream. Then another shouted. She saw the people turn and stare in amazement at the stampede. She was right in the midst of it; would she be noticed among the animals?

Then a voice rose up from the knot. A voice she knew so well. 'GO! Follow *them*! Animals ALWAYS know the way to safety!'

It was her mother—taking control. She was grabbing the arms of people around her and thrusting them forward, yelling 'GO! GO! GO!' And the people *were* going. Tima glanced back over her shoulder as the stag plunged on down the slope. Around its hoofs swarmed hundreds, *thousands* of small furry creatures. She felt overcome with gratitude. These animals did not need to do this. Most of them could find safety in their own territory. They were simply putting on an incredible show—just to guide the humans to the safe side of the valley.

Now twenty or so people from the holiday park were racing after them. Tima glanced back and thought she caught her father's perplexed expression for an instant. Had he seen her? A minute later she was too far ahead of the fleeing holidaymakers to be identified. She had to focus all her attention on not falling off. She knew there was a reason why man had never ridden deer; they were so damned uncomfortable compared to horses!

She thought of Elena ... where *was* she? As they reached the safe side of the loch, Tima's stag came to a halt and she slid off. She turned to see the crowd of people running full pelt, just a minute away. Amongst them she saw the blonde ponytail of her friend, bouncing along. Elena had caught up with the people and joined them.

Tima let out a heavy sigh of relief. Then there was another tremendous rumble and two of the village lodges slid into the loch. On the horizon a rescue helicopter was already heading in; one of many circling the mountains these past two days. Tima closed her eyes and *willed* the grubs to push on with their tunnel-propping duties.

As the people approached, the animals dispersed and Tima went with them, riding the stag until she reached a natural outcrop where she could dismount and stay out of sight. A short distance away, Elena peeled quietly away from the traumatized holidaymakers, safely huddled on the opposite slope to the ruined village, and came to find her. Guided by rabbits, she turned the corner of the outcrop and dropped down next to Tima with a shaky sigh, still puffing.

'Well done,' said Tima, giving her a hug. 'But now we've got to get back inside the mountain, find Queenie, and get the last grubs home!'

Elena groaned into her hands. 'How are we ever going to do it in time?'

'We have to travel by antler express,' said Tima, indicating the *two* stags who now stood nearby, at the ready.

'But I'm too heavy!' wailed Elena. 'And I'll fall off.'

'No—he's strong. He can stand it for a quick sprint. And just do like I do!' said Tima.

Elena rolled her eyes. 'Well, I guess if I've ridden an alien rock-eating worm, this should be easy . . .'

CHAPTER 44

'Yesss! They've done it!' Matt punched the air and showed Jamie the console. The last area of red flashing warning light had now switched off. As they watched, the final stretch of tunnels turned steadily from pale pink to blue; all now safely propped. Finally, the last three white dots began to make their way back to Grub Central.

Jamie had seen off all the other creatures by now and had been waiting, anxiously, with Matt for the past twenty minutes. He looked at his watch and gulped. 'Are they going to get back in time?'

Matt glanced up at him. He didn't look too hopeful. 'Look . . . we've got rid of *most* of them. And maybe just four left behind won't be so bad.'

'They breed,' said Jamie, giving Matt a stony look.

'Ah,' said Matt.

'And they have no natural predator,' Jamie went on.

'Fair point,' said Matt.

'And the only way humans can stop them is—I don't know—probably to nuke the mountains. Which they probably will, once they realize there are aliens infesting them.'

Matt took a deep breath and looked back down at the console. 'They'll get here. Just be ready.'

Jamie couldn't be certain how precise the countdown was, but, when Elena and Tima finally brought the convoy of grubs in, he reckoned they were down to their last ten minutes.

'Get on! Get ON!' bawled Elena, as soon as they were in view. Queenie barely slowed down while Matt helped Jamie scramble aboard and then leapt up after him. They took the last stretch of tunnel at an amazing speed, the lost grubs now so close they were bumping each other.

'They know they're running out of time!' yelled Tima. 'They want to join the others. They're terrified of being left behind.'

Jamie glanced at the console, wedged under Matt's arm. He could still see the green light of the inter-dimensional shaft indicated on its screen. The exit was still there. But it could wink out at any moment.

They reached the cave at record speed and once again, Queenie pulled aside to let the others go on ahead. Jamie jumped down and ran in after them to send them on their way. Neither of them paused to be nervous, he noticed. They steamed on into the green shaft, one after the other, rings of teeth nudging footplates . . . and were gone.

There was a moment of quiet as the dandelion beams of light spun around. Then a gentle whistle and Queenie rolled around the corner and into the beam cave, ready to take the last ticket to the moon. Tima hopped off the footplate and ran around to the front to press her forehead against the grub's single eye. 'Thank you,' she said, tears on her face. 'Thank you SO much.'

'Um,' said Matt. 'Before she goes . . . there's just one more thing. We need to protect this cave. We need to ask her to do that thing they do . . . you know . . . make a rock wall.'

'What—seal it up?' said Tima.

'Yeah,' said Matt. 'You know there will be people coming down to check out all these caves and tunnels once they find them. Earthquake scientists and all that. They'll find the prop fungus and they'll find the canisters . . . and I don't care about that, but . . .'

'. . . but imagine if they found *this*,' concluded Elena, gazing with something like love at the beam post.

'So . . . are we all going on the other side, while she seals herself in?' asked Tima. 'And then hoping she'll be in time to just go on alone?' She didn't look happy.

'No—*we're* getting sealed in too,' said Matt. 'So we can send her on her way.'

'Um . . . we're getting sealed *in*?' said Elena. 'Really?'

Matt grinned. 'Not really,' he said. 'There's another way out. It's always been here. The grubs made that hole.' He waved towards the tunnel beyond the edge of the cave's natural shape. 'It was never here before. That . . .' he pointed up to a smooth chimney of rock to his left, '. . . is where you're supposed to get in and out of here. It'll be a bit of a climb, but we can do it. Lucky's already checked it out.'

Tima pressed her forehead to Queenie's one final time. The grub did a U-turn and went out to the edge of the naturally-formed cave. Its spinning teeth retracted and a strange metallic proboscis emerged from beneath its single eye. Then it turned to the tunnel entrance and set to work with a low grinding noise. They couldn't see exactly how it mended the hole, but it was done incredibly fast. Two minutes later Queenie powered down, gently reversed, and turned back to face them. The rock wall looked—and felt—as if it had always been there.

They all walked alongside as Queenie trundled towards the green beam. Each of them pressed a hand to her skin and sent in a thank you. Even Jamie could feel it as the grub sent something back to them too . . . a kind of gratitude of its own. Because it was going to join its family and roam free, happily honeycombing an alien moon with perfectly round tunnels.

A few seconds later it was gone. And a few seconds after that, so was the green beam.

'That,' said Elena, 'was *close.*'

Jamie turned to look at the spiralling chimney of rock that led up from their cave.

'I hope Lucky's right about that exit,' he said. 'Or we've just entombed ourselves.'

CHAPTER 45

It was only mid morning as they reached the surface. The climb had been very hard—twisting and steep. Their exit seemed to have been formed out of some kind of slippery, waxy rock; like a natural helter-skelter. Each of them had slid back down it at some point, cannoning into anyone below and causing a small avalanche of exhausted climbers.

In the end, Matt asked Lucky to fly on ahead and steer him towards the safest bits to climb; some areas were rougher to the touch and offered better grip. Then Matt led the way, the handy head torch on his forehead helping him to follow Lucky's guidance. The rest of them climbed in his path, feeling out the safest grips in the rock. Tima was impressed that Jamie kept up with them all with no complaint. She was exhausted by the long climb, and she was a dancer and pretty fit. Jamie, with his weak left side, must have found it much harder—but he had still managed it. These Highlanders were made of tough stuff. But this didn't surprise her so much; she had learned that her new friend was incredibly brave and resilient.

It took them all nearly twenty minutes to get up but at last they saw a narrow, low opening ahead of them, Lucky flying in and out of it with obvious excitement and relief. They had to push themselves along on their bellies to get through the gap, which was shaped like a wide smile in the rock, before they found themselves out on the freezing mountainside in a snowstorm.

Tima was almost ready to dig a hole and crawl into it, she was so tired, but Jamie climbed out behind her, stood up straight, stretching his tired limbs, and then headed off down the mountain on a very definite path. It was an immense relief to realize he knew exactly where they were. 'Everyone!' he called out. 'Hold on to each other. You're too tired to take any risks on the climb down.'

Tima reached for Jamie's hand, and Elena's just behind her. Later, she wondered if she had actually fallen asleep on her feet after that because she had no memory of their journey. It took them at least half an hour, carefully working their way down through the snow, just to reach the road.

'Hang on a minute!' yelled Matt, as they reached a winding road. The snow had stopped and a car was visible on the verge.

'It's Uncle Fraser!' yelled Jamie. 'He's come out to find us!'

Uncle Fraser was angry. He was also hugely relieved. 'I can't *believe* you all went out again—in all THIS!' he yelled at them as they stumbled towards the Jeep. 'Earthquakes all over the mountains. What were you thinking?!'

They all got into the car and found they had nothing to say as relief and exhaustion hit them.

Finally Jamie said: 'It's OK. No more earthquakes. It's over.'

Uncle Fraser started up the engine and drove back towards home. 'Did you just say there'll be no more earthquakes, Jamie?' he said.

'Yeah, that's what he said,' murmured Tima, her head sliding down onto Elena's shoulder. 'Don't worry. We sorted it all out.'

'Oh great,' said Uncle Fraser. 'It's always good to be a taxi service for superheroes.'

CHAPTER 46

Ellie—I know you're doing something good, Mum had texted. But I miss you. It's OK—I'm not ill again. I am taking all my meds. I just want my girl back. When are you coming home?

I think it will be tonight. Most of the roads are open again, Elena replied. I will call you soon, I promise. xxx

The satellite masts had obviously been properly fixed now, because at last their phones worked.

'We'll drop Tima off first, OK?' Fraser said. He pulled up a narrow road and headed towards a group of chalets high in the peaks. This was where a number of local tourists had been taken after their holiday homes had been hit by the earthquakes. Tima had been on the phone to her parents for some time back at Jamie's place.

They'd all had a lunch of chicken stew, eating in exhausted

silence, before news came through that the roads had been made passable in most places. Fraser had agreed to take them out again, after they'd had a couple of hours sleep—Tima to reunite with her parents, and Matt and Elena to see if a car journey home was still an option.

Jamie was riding with them. He still hadn't told his uncle and granddad much about what had happened . . . and Elena wasn't sure how much they would understand . . . or believe. It was OK, though. Whatever Jamie wanted to say . . . it was OK.

'Any messages?' she asked Matt, noticing him checking his phone.

He grimaced and handed over his mobile. The tiny screen was full of messages from his mum, all increasingly frantic. The last one read: **Matt—the police came. The owner of the Land Rover called them. He wouldn't wait any longer.**

Matt had texted back: **I will see you soon. x**

Elena noticed he hadn't added: **Don't worry—it'll be OK.** Because it wouldn't be.

CHAPTER 47

'Oh thank heavens!'

Tima braced herself for the impact of her mum and dad as they ran to hug her. By the door of their new—safe—holiday lodge, Jamie and Fraser hung back as she was swept into her parents' embrace.

'I will NEVER bring you to Scotland again!' Mum promised, fiercely, into her hair. 'It's SO dangerous! We're taking you home right now!'

'No!' protested Tima. 'I've got a show to do in Edinburgh! I can't drop out! It's bad enough I've missed two days of rehearsals.'

'I think they'll understand,' said Dad, holding her away and checking her over for signs of damage. 'After all, the Highland earthquakes have been all over the news!'

'They're all finished now,' said Tima. 'We'll be fine.'

'There's no way we're staying here,' insisted Mum. 'We'll book into a hotel in Edinburgh if we must but we're getting out of these mountains and never coming back.' She became aware of Jamie and his uncle just a few steps away, and looked suddenly mortified. 'I'm so sorry,' she said, her hands at her throat. 'This is your home. I—it's just I've been so scared. It's very selfish of me not to think of you. And we are so grateful that you've kept Tima safe with you.'

'No trouble,' said Fraser, smiling and resting his hand on Jamie's shoulder. 'We've loved having her.' Tima smiled at him gratefully; he hadn't given away that she'd been AWOL all night long. 'It's been . . . very entertaining,' he added.

'Oh no—don't tell me she started chatting to spiders!' said Mum, rolling her eyes. 'She does that kind of thing.'

Tima disentangled herself from her parents and went over to Jamie. 'I will come back,' she said, quietly. 'To see you. I promise. And . . . you and your uncle and granddad must come to see the show. I will get tickets for you all. Will you come?'

Jamie nodded. 'I wouldn't miss it,' he said, grinning.

'Well, we'd better get going,' said Fraser. 'Things to do.' He glanced at his nephew with narrowed eyes. 'Chats to have.'

There was more effusive thanks from her parents but Tima just gave Jamie a long hug. After a few seconds of mild shock he hugged her back. Very quietly he said: 'You changed my life. You changed . . . me. I'm almost . . .'

'. . . cool,' said Tima. 'But not almost. *Totally* cool. See you soon, Sandpaper Boy.'

As soon as they had left, Mum and Dad made sweet spiced tea and told her all about their earthquake adventures. 'The most amazing thing,' Mum said, 'was when all these animals started stampeding down the mountainside and we realized they were making for the safest ground—so we followed them to the far side of the loch. Seconds later half the holiday village fell into the mountain. Those animals saved our lives!'

'It was incredible,' said Dad. 'You should have been there.'

'But we were so glad you were not!' added Mum. 'It's been a great comfort to know that you've been safe and sound in a cosy little crofter's cottage for the last two days. I bet you were bored, though, weren't you? No internet or phone calls. How did you manage?'

'Oh,' said Tima. 'We passed the time.'

Miraculously the Land Rover was completely undamaged by the earthquakes—and by the emergency road crews. It had been bumped to the verge to make way for trucks, which had brought in slabs of concrete and iron to make temporary road bridges across the breaks. The road was declared safe on local radio not long before Uncle Fraser agreed to drive Tima to her parents, so he was able to take Matt and Elena on to their car afterwards.

'Well . . . I don't quite know what to say to you both,' said Uncle Fraser, turning around in his seat as the Jeep engine idled. 'I hope whatever you were doing all night was worth it.'

'It was,' said Matt. 'There haven't been any more earthquakes.'

Uncle Fraser nodded and Jamie said to Elena and Matt:

'I'm going to tell him—all of it. Is that OK? I mean . . . all the tunnels and the prop fungus . . . it's all going to be found, sooner or later, isn't it?'

'That's fine,' said Elena. 'Tell him all of it. Just . . . wait until we've gone, OK? And . . . if you can edit us out, if anyone else wants to know about it, that'd be great.'

Uncle Fraser, hearing Elena's side quite clearly, shrugged, rolled his eyes, and replied: 'You were never here.' He reached across to stroke Lucky's feathers as she perched on Matt's shoulder. 'This has been . . . weird.'

Jamie grinned. 'I'll tell him slooooowly,' he said. 'So he understands. He might even believe it.'

'Whatever he tells you,' said Elena, giving Uncle Fraser a hard stare. 'It's true. It's all true.'

Then she leaned over and gave Jamie a hug and a kiss. Matt shook his hand and the pair of them jumped out and walked across to the Land Rover, Lucky fluttering just above their heads.

Uncle Fraser waited until they started up the car and then he turned the Jeep around and headed for home.

'Are you going to tell me the whole story now?' he asked, glancing over at his nephew.

'When we're home,' said Jamie. 'I will need to draw.'

Uncle Fraser nodded, looking intrigued but managing to keep a lid on his curiosity. 'Are you, OK?' he asked.

Jamie settled back in his seat as the car paused for a few deer to cross the road. Several of them paused and looked his way. He gave them a little wave and they tossed their heads in response and then went on down the mountainside, disappearing in flurries of snow.

'Never better,' said Jamie.

CHAPTER 48

It was fully dark as they reached Doncaster. Elena had slept for a part of the journey, slumped against the window with her bag as a pillow. She felt guilty when she woke up, knowing Matt was every bit as exhausted as she was. She should make an effort to stay awake and talk to him.

But Matt didn't seem to want to talk.

'Matt—what are you going to do?' she asked, pushing her hair out of her eyes and blinking the sleep away.

'What do you think I'm going to do?' he muttered. 'Take the car back. Probably give it a wash.'

He was being flippant. Deliberately not going there. Elena sighed. 'You can stay at mine; you know that. Mum's already said it will be fine. If you need to.'

Matt shrugged. 'Got to go home sooner or later,' he said.

'Even if it's just to get my things.'

Elena couldn't imagine what kind of reception Matt was going to get. Actually, she *could* imagine it. She just didn't want to. Despite all the good they had just done, he was never going to get a break. She was filled with dread for what lay ahead for him.

'Let's get coffee and doughnuts,' said Matt, abruptly veering into a motorway services. 'You can go in and get them while I put a bit more fuel in.'

Elena nodded. As soon as Matt pulled up at the petrol pump she slipped out of the car and went into the shop. She remembered how they'd be paying for the fuel and made a guilty mental note to post that wallet as soon as she could. She wasn't sure how much money she could get to replace the cash, though. That might have to wait a bit longer; she'd just send it anonymously when she could.

Before she went to the coffee machine she decided to nip into the toilet. She found a grimy cubicle with a high open window. A cold winter breeze was blasting through it as she washed her hands.

'Don't come back.'

Elena glanced up, startled, to see Lucky sitting on the sill above her. The voice she was copying was unmistakable. Matt's.

'Don't come back,' the bird repeated and then flew away.

Elena flung open the toilet door and raced out into the shop. Even before she reached the window she could see the blue and red lights whirling across the forecourt.

'Whoa! It's all kicking off out there!' said the young man on the till, gawping out through the glass.

Elena peered through a gap between a display of maps and a chiller cabinet and choked back a cry of alarm, both hands across her mouth. Outside were two police cars and four officers. One of them had Matt up against the side of the Land Rover, his hands over his head, face pressed to its rear window.

'Oh dear, *someone's* in trouble,' went on the man at the till. He obviously hadn't seen which car she'd climbed out of.

Elena swallowed a sob. She wanted to run out there. She wanted to flail her arms in the faces of the officers. She wanted to scream: 'LEAVE him ALONE! He's just done something AMAZING and saved loads of lives! Like he always does! Like he always does!'

Over the past few months Matt had been so brave. So steady. So *heroic* . . . but nobody could ever know how. Or why. So he was going to get arrested for car theft. And that wasn't the worst of it. What he would get from his violent father was the worst of it.

There was only one thing she could do for him now.

Not come back.

Elena gulped. Took a deep breath. Went to buy doughnuts. At the till she asked: 'Do you know where the nearest train station is?'

'Erm . . . Hatfield and Stainforth is nearest,' said the man, handing over her change. 'About 15 minutes in the car.'

'Is it walkable?' she asked.

He shrugged. 'Maybe. Not sure. It's no distance as the crow flies. Just through the woods and over the fields.' He waved vaguely through the window and Elena tried not to watch as Matt was put into the back of a patrol car. 'Wouldn't try it in the dark, though, love.'

'Thanks,' she said. 'Just wondered.'

She stepped outside the shop and turned along the side of the brick building. Beyond the wide car park, the shopping area, and the budget chain hotel, were trees—looming black. No normal girl would seek a route through the woods in the dead of night. But she was a Night Speaker and this was her time.

She made for the trees and the help she knew she would find there. She didn't look back.

CHAPTER 49

Matt woke at 12.34 a.m. just as the beam went through. He wondered how fast it travelled between here and the cave where they'd said goodbye to Queenie. Of all the places in Thornleigh, he would not have guessed that the police station custody suite would have been on the path of the beam. The station—his final destination after a relay of police escorts from Doncaster— occupied a modest corner of the Thornleigh Town Hall building. It was on a line which travelled through his house and Elena's and Tima's, then here . . . and on through the Quarry End industrial estate and into Leigh Hill.

The beam passed through quite high . . . across the ceiling. It sang its beautiful song and filled him with familiar longing. He guessed nobody else here had seen it.

Maybe if just one Thornleigh adult *had* been able to see it, he might have had some chance of explaining the things he'd done; the petty crimes he had committed this year. He might have had some chance of convincing everyone that it had been the only way; that they would have done the same.

The beam left behind a sweetness that faded to grey. Matt lay on the hard metal bunk and watched the stars through the high window, open just a hand's width. A small shadow arrived on the sill. 'Come on then,' said Matt.

Lucky landed on his head. She would keep him company until dawn when the duty solicitor arrived. He would be sure to send her safely back through the window before anyone stepped inside his cell.

'It's good to see you,' he whispered, stroking her feathers. 'Jailbird.'

'Jailbird,' she said back.

ACKNOWLEDGEMENTS

With grateful thanks to my go to earth scientist, Dr Simon Boxall, for guidance on earthquakes. There will always be more questions . . .

And thanks, as ever, to the brilliant Liz Cross and Debbie Sims, for making me make this a better book.

ALI SPARKES

Ali Sparkes was a journalist and BBC broadcaster until she chucked in the safe job to go dangerously freelance and try her hand at writing comedy scripts. Her first venture was as a comedy columnist on *Woman's Hour* and later on *Home Truths*. Not long after, she discovered her real love was writing children's fiction.

Ali grew up adoring adventure stories about kids who mess about in the woods and still likes to mess about in the woods herself whenever possible. She lives with her husband and two sons in Southampton, England.

HAVE YOU READ THEM ALL?